The sound of the galloping horse drew near...

"Aurelia!"

"Marcus!" sh_____ce. He was the on_____e was searching for_____toward his voice.

"What in heaven's name are you doing out here?" Marcus called to her, guiding her with his voice.

"I heard crying in the night." To her delight, she saw a glimmer of light. She moved toward it through the thorn trees. At last she saw Marcus, riding his horse, Cogar. "Thank goodness you decided to ride this way."

"I came to check on you. When your car was at the cottage and you weren't, I became concerned."

"It's a good thing you did," Aurelia said. "I was lost." Marcus held down his hand, and she jumped up behind him, her body snug against his strong back. "I heard the horse's hooves, and I thought the ghost was coming. But it was you, coming to rescue me."

Dear Harlequin Intrigue Reader,

Spring is in the air…and so is mystery. And just as always, Harlequin Intrigue has a spectacular lineup of breathtaking romantic suspense for you to enjoy.

Continuing her oh-so-sexy HEROES INC. trilogy, Susan Kearney brings us *Defending the Heiress*—which should say it all. As if anyone *wouldn't* want to be personally protected by a hunk!

Veteran Harlequin Intrigue author Caroline Burnes has crafted a super Southern gothic miniseries. THE LEGEND OF BLACKTHORN has everything—skeletons in the closet, a cast of unique characters and even a handsome masked phantom who rides a black stallion. And can he kiss! *Rider in the Mist* is the first of two classic tales.

The Cradle Mission by Rita Herron is another installment in her NIGHTHAWK ISLAND series. This time a cop has to protect his dead brother's baby and the beautiful woman left to care for the child. But why is someone dead set on rocking the cradle…?

Finally, Sylvie Kurtz leads us down into one woman's horror—so deep, she's all but unreachable…until she meets and trusts one man to lead her out of the darkness in *Under Lock and Key*.

We hope you savor all four titles and return again next month for more exciting stories.

Sincerely,

Denise O'Sullivan
Senior Editor
Harlequin Intrigue

RIDER IN THE MIST
CAROLINE BURNES

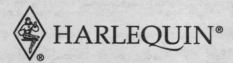

HARLEQUIN®

TORONTO • NEW YORK • LONDON
AMSTERDAM • PARIS • SYDNEY • HAMBURG
STOCKHOLM • ATHENS • TOKYO • MILAN • MADRID
PRAGUE • WARSAW • BUDAPEST • AUCKLAND

ISBN 0-373-22711-6

RIDER IN THE MIST

Visit us at www.eHarlequin.com

Printed in U.S.A.

ABOUT THE AUTHOR

Caroline Burnes continues her life as doorman and can opener for her six cats and three dogs. E. A. Poe, the prototype cat for Familiar, rules as king of the ranch, followed by his lieutenants, Miss Vesta, Gumbo, Chester, Maggie the Cat and Ash. The dogs, though a more lowly life form, are tolerated as foot soldiers by the cats. They are Sweetie Pie, Maybelline and Corky.

Books by Caroline Burnes

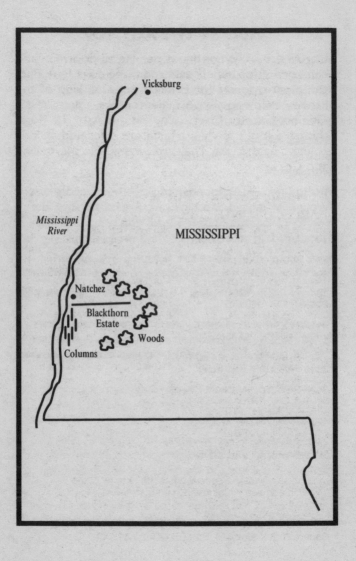

CAST OF CHARACTERS

Aurelia Agee—When Aurelia learns that her incapacitated mother is heir to an estate in Natchez, Mississippi, she goes to sell the estate—only to discover that the past doesn't rest easy on the acres of Blackthorn.

Marcus McNeese—His love of history and his desire to preserve Blackthorn puts him at odds with Aurelia.

Andre Agee—The founder of Blackthorn, Andre was wrongfully hanged as a highwayman shortly after the War Between the States. But his ghost still rides the woods of Blackthorn on the devil horse Diable.

Joey Reynolds—Once the son of the caretaker of Blackthorn, Joey shows up in the woods at the most inappropriate times. Is there a reason he searches the woods?

Yvonne Harris—One of the best real estate agents in Natchez, Yvonne is determined to help Aurelia sell the old estate, for a handsome commission—until she has a ghostly encounter.

Leon Kimball—Leon has big dreams for Blackthorn—as a shopping mecca. Is he greedy enough to kill for a profit?

Randall Levert—Randall has his hands full with his car dealership and his crazy mother, but is he also manipulating events in the hopes of laying claim to Blackthorn?

Lottie Levert—Claiming to be an illegitimate heir to Blackthorn, Lottie causes trouble wherever she goes.

Chapter One

Aurelia Agee pulled the collar of her coat tighter. It was normally cold in Minnesota in February, but somehow she'd expected a balmier welcome in Mississippi. Like all of her other expectations, this one was wrong. The wind blowing off the Mississippi River was bitter cold, and the storm clouds gathering in the west promised wind, rain and lightning. It was not an auspicious beginning to her quest.

Shivering, she stared up at the eighteen columns that stretched into a sky growing dark. Tragic. That was the word that came to her mind. The columns were all that remained of her family's Natchez, Mississippi, estate—except for the shame. Now, a century and a half later, the shame lingered. She bit her bottom lip. How was it possible that she could feel any responsibility for the actions taken by a man who died on a gallows in 1869? A man—though he was her great-great-great-grandfather—she'd never even heard of until recently. That, at least, was in keeping with the little she knew about the man who was listed on her birth certificate as her father. Serge Agee had abandoned his wife and infant daughter without so much as a farewell. It had come as a big surprise to her and her mother to discover they were heirs to an Agee family estate in Mississippi.

Aurelia walked along the high bluffs of the river. In the daylight, it would be a magnificent view. In the gathering dusk it was positively eerie. Blackthorn had once been a thriving estate. The fertile land had produced some of the finest cotton grown in the South. Andre Agee had supplemented his income by donning a mask and becoming a highwayman on the stretch of road from Nashville to New Orleans known as the Natchez Trace. Yvonne Harris, a local Realtor, had told Aurelia a few of the stories that were part of his legend in Natchez. Andre had ridden a huge black horse and he'd come thundering out of the woods with his sword drawn. No traveler was safe from the diabolical highwayman who seemed to take pleasure in terrifying his victims.

Until he was caught and hanged.

Yvonne had been somewhat gleeful in recounting how the townspeople had built a gallows right on Blackthorn Estate and hung him on his own property.

That was why Blackthorn was haunted. The ghost of Andre Agee still rode the unkempt fields and forests of his old home.

Yvonne Harris had been a great source of information, until she'd abruptly quit, which was why Aurelia had decided to come to Natchez and sell the estate herself.

Shoving her hands in her pockets against the cold, Aurelia found the key that would unlock the caretaker's cottage. That was where she'd stay until she made arrangements to sell Blackthorn Estate. Then with the money in hand, she'd return to Minnesota with enough funds to pay her mother's nursing home care.

She heard the sound of the car long before the headlights broke through the thick woods that surrounded the old estate. Surprised, she waited for the Mercedes SUV to stop. The tall, good-looking man who stepped out from behind the wheel came straight toward her.

"Leon Kimball," he said, holding out his hand. "I heard the heir to the Agee estate was in town, but I certainly didn't expect her to be so…"

"Young?" Aurelia asked with sarcasm. She was only twenty-two, but she'd borne the responsibilities of an adult since her mother's illness had robbed Ursula of her mental capacity.

"Young, yes, but I was going to say beautiful." He continued to hold out his hand and Aurelia finally shook it.

"I'm a local attorney," Leon said. "I heard you were going to put Blackthorn on the market. I'd like to make an offer. I want to tell you I've been trying to buy it for back taxes, but now that the rightful heir is here, I'm willing to make a fair offer."

Aurelia felt the first flush of relief. She'd been in town less than four hours and she had an offer, despite what the Realtor had told her. "Yes, I'm going to sell the estate. But I thought there was no local interest?" As soon as the words were out of her mouth, she realized what a mistake they were. If this man was interested, she'd all but told him no one else was.

Leon only laughed. "Blackthorn does have something of a reputation." He glanced behind her at the bluffs that overlooked the Mississippi River. "A lot of people believe the place is haunted. I understand Yvonne Harris came out here to put up a For Sale sign and had something of a fright."

"She refused to give me any details, so I'm not certain what actually happened," Aurelia said.

Leon leaned closer and lowered his voice. "She was walking through the woods and she heard someone following her. Whoever it was pursued her through the woods. I can tell you as an eyewitness, she was scratched up pretty good from running through tree limbs and brambles."

"Probably a squirrel rustling through the fallen leaves," Aurelia said with a hint of contempt. "After all these years, you'd think people wouldn't believe in ghost stories."

"Not just ghost stories," Leon said, giving her a wide smile. "Yvonne isn't the kind of woman to be frightened by rodents. She's quite determined, under normal circumstances. You should know that I sent a contractor out here several weeks ago to assess the property for development. He walked around the estate and when he returned, someone had let the air out of all of his tires. He found a devil's walking stick beside his car.''

"A what?" Aurelia tried to ignore the tingle of flesh at her neck. Despite the fact that she didn't believe in ghosts or spirits, Leon Kimball was getting to her.

"It's a type of tree with thorns all over it. There's a thicket on the estate. I believe that's where the Blackthorn name derived from.''

"Fascinating,'' Aurelia said with sarcasm. "But this sounds like made-up tales to lower the price of Blackthorn. I can assure you those tactics won't work.''

Leon laughed and shook his head. "The local teenagers insist that Andre Agee rides the premises on his black stallion, Diable, straight from the gates of hell.''

"Of course the local ghost would ride a black stallion with the French name for devil.'' Aurelia had no interest in local bogeymen, especially if they might drive off a prospective buyer for the estate. "That's such a cliché I can't imagine how anyone could believe it.''

"A cliché, perhaps, but the teenagers swear they've seen the horse. They say he's huge, with flowing mane and tail. And red eyes. Diable. Nothing less would serve for the Fantôme.'' Leon gave the name the French pronunciation and followed it with a laugh. "You aren't impressed with local history, I see."

"History, yes. High school fabrication, no."

Leon looked up at the old columns. "It's getting late, Miss Agee. Shall I follow you back into town?"

"I'm staying here." Aurelia felt no need to tell him that her financial situation wouldn't allow for a hotel room in town. The caretaker's cottage would be free.

"Alone?" Leon looked shocked. "Out here?"

"I live alone in Minneapolis," Aurelia said dryly. "And I'm not afraid of ghosts."

"I wouldn't tempt Andre," Leon warned her with a twinkle. "It was said he never injured a lady in his robberies, but he didn't hesitate to take their jewels and money."

"Yes, my great-great-great-grandfather, the local highwayman," Aurelia said. "Hung as a thief. A lovely heritage."

"All families have their black sheep," Leon said. "Yours is just very colorful."

Aurelia didn't find her family history colorful or entertaining. "Let me get settled in, Mr. Kimball. Tomorrow I'd like to talk to you about Blackthorn. I need to get the land appraised—"

"Then you will entertain my offer?" Leon's eyes held hope.

Aurelia didn't hesitate. She'd come to sell the property, and here was a buyer. "I'd be delighted to entertain your proposal, as long as it's a fair one."

"Let's put business behind us for the evening,"

Leon said. "Let me take you to dinner tonight. Natchez has some wonderful restaurants and a marvelous history."

"I don't know...." Aurelia was starving but she had no intention of trying to cook in the cottage.

"Madeline's has the most wonderful trout. Very light, perfectly seasoned."

Aurelia could almost taste the fish. "Dinner would be lovely," she capitulated.

"I'll pick you up at seven," Leon said as he walked to his car. "Be careful at Blackthorn, Miss Agee. There may not be ghosts, but the estate is old. There are wells and any number of other places that could be dangerous."

"I'll watch my step," Aurelia said, feeling again the tingle of apprehension.

MARCUS McNEESE leaned forward in the cowhide rocker and watched the sky darken over the river. He could just catch a glimpse of the dying sunlight on a bend of the mighty Mississippi. A cold breeze was blowing off the river and a storm was brewing in the west. Such weather could bode ill in February. Natchez didn't see a lot of snow, but a wet February storm could bring plenty of misery.

As if he didn't have enough.

He saw the slender young woman walk out of the trees before she saw him. As she came toward him, he studied her heavy coat, gloves and hat. She was dressed for cold weather. No surprise since she came from Minnesota. She was younger than he'd expected. And prettier. In fact, she was downright beautiful with her dark curly hair and her pale skin.

"Miss Agee," he said when she was ten yards away. Even so, he startled her, and he could see that she didn't like being surprised.

"Who are you?" she demanded. "And what are you doing on my porch?" Her glance strayed to the two suitcases sitting beside the door as if she thought he might steal them.

"Waiting for you," he said, taking the steps to the ground so that he stood in front of her. "My name is Marcus McNeese. I have a television repair shop in town."

"I'm not interested in a TV. I won't be here long enough to need one," she said.

"I came to talk to you about Blackthorn."

He had her attention.

"What about Blackthorn? Are you interested in buying it?"

"As much as I'd like to own the property, I'm not here to make an offer. But I understand you're going to sell the estate. I'm here to ask you not to do that." He could see her brownish-green eyes harden and he knew he was bungling the meeting.

"It's mine to sell, or I should say my mother's. I'm acting on her behalf and we've firmly decided to sell."

"Perhaps I could speak with your mother," he

said, wishing he knew more about the beautiful and angry woman standing in front of him.

"If only you could. I'd like to speak to her, too. The problem is that she doesn't seem to hear anyone. She has Alzheimer's disease."

He saw the tears then, before she blinked them away. "I'm sorry. I'm making a mess of this."

"What is it that you want?" Aurelia said.

"I'd like to ask you not to sell Blackthorn to someone who'll develop the property. It's of tremendous historic value. Blackthorn Estate played a major role in the development of this area. Andre Agee was one of the first Mississippians to free his slaves. He provided living space for the Native Americans on his land, and there's a major burial mound on the property. If a developer gets this land, all of this will be destroyed to build another mall that no one wants or needs."

Aurelia stood without moving. "So you want me to keep the property for the sake of history."

"That or sell it to someone who will."

"Do you have a buyer with such interests?" she asked.

"Not at the moment."

"Mr. McNeese, I intend to sell Blackthorn to the first person who offers me what it's worth. I don't care if that's a historian or a developer. I can't afford to care."

She walked past him, up the steps and to the front

door of the cottage. "Please get off my property." She walked inside and slammed the door.

AURELIA LEANED AGAINST the heavy wooden door and let the air out of her lungs. She'd been in Natchez less than four hours and already two men had been on her property.

Her property. She savored the words. In Minneapolis, she rented. She'd never been able to come up with the down payment for a home. Now she discovered she was heir to nearly a thousand acres of an old plantation and the guest cottage. A beautiful estate, under all the neglect. It wouldn't take much imagination to visualize the place as it once had been, a showplace.

She looked around the caretaker's cottage. It was snug and quaint, actually perfect for her. The windows looked out on a view of the forest to the west and the river bluffs to the east. When it was better light, she wanted to walk along the bluffs and enjoy the view of the Mississippi River. She remembered from grammar school history that the Indian name meant "father of waters."

At the thought of history, Marcus McNeese popped back into her mind. Damn he was an arrogant man, coming up and asking her not to sell the property because he thought it had historical value. Well, if some historical society wanted Blackthorn, she'd be glad to sell it to them, as long as they were the high bidder.

What Marcus McNeese didn't understand, and would never know, was that she couldn't keep Blackthorn even if she wanted to. Her mother was so very ill, and the little money they'd saved was gone. She needed the proceeds from Blackthorn to keep her mother comfortable in a nursing facility where she could receive the best care.

Aurelia retrieved her suitcases and put them on the bed to unpack. She forced her thoughts to the coming dinner with Leon Kimball. It was a stroke of luck that he'd driven up, especially since her Realtor had proven to be such a 'fraidy cat. Yvonne Harris had been so badly frightened she'd called up and quit. But it seemed folks around Natchez were a lot more susceptible to ghost stories than folks in Minnesota.

Leon wasn't the kind of man who could be easily frightened away, and that might just work to her advantage. He said he wanted Blackthorn to develop.

Even as she thought it, she felt a pang. Blackthorn was beautiful. Most of the fields had grown up in scrub trees and weeds, but the forest around the old ruins was magnificent. The hardwood trees seemed to stretch into the sky. They were virgin growth. It would be a shame for them all to be bulldozed. But Aurelia realized she couldn't afford to get sentimental about trees when her mother's comfort depended on the sale of the property. Besides, it was technically her mother's land. She was only acting as agent, doing what was in her mother's best interest.

Sighing, she took out a green sweater and black

slacks. Leon hadn't given any indication of appropriate attire, and she hadn't even checked to see if the telephone in the cottage had been turned on as she'd ordered. She picked up the receiver and got a loud dial tone. Well, that was one thing going her way.

The bathroom in the cottage contained no shower but an old claw-foot tub that was deep enough to swim in. She ran the tub full of hot water and slowly sank into it.

As she closed her eyes, she saw again Marcus McNeese step off the porch and into the yard. He was a tall man. At least six foot four. He looked more like a manual laborer than a television repairman. She smiled at the idea of his large hands working on the delicate computer board of a television. He just didn't seem right for the job, but she didn't know why.

He was a handsome man. Nordic looking with his blond hair and blue eyes. And there was something so gentle about him. Too bad he wanted the impossible.

The ringing of the telephone startled her. She hopped out of the tub, wrapping a towel around her as she ran to the phone.

"Hello," she said, wondering who could be calling her.

There was only the sound of breathing on the line.

"Who is this?" she asked, anger making her voice sharp.

Again there was only breathing.

"I'm reporting this to the phone company," she said, slamming the phone down in the cradle.

Her hand hovered over it for a moment as she contemplated calling the phone company. Wasn't it just her luck? Her first caller was obscene. With her hand on the dial, she hesitated. Everyone in town was already talking about her. Wouldn't it be perfect if the rumor got around that she was being harassed? That would surely drive any other potential buyers away. Well, she wasn't going to play into anyone's hands.

She put on her clothes and got ready for Leon to arrive. When she was dressed and had applied some lipstick, she walked out on the front porch.

The sky was thick with clouds, but on occasion, the moon broke through, gilding the oyster-shell drive with white light. She walked down the drive toward the old ruins of the plantation. It was about two hundred yards from the cottage, but she had plenty of time.

When she could just make out the pillars jutting into the night sky she stopped. This was her heritage. If circumstances were different, she might have moved to Natchez and tried to do something with the land. It was said to be some of the most fertile in the world.

What would it be like to own a thousand acres, she wondered as she gazed at the old pillars.

From behind her she heard the sound of something striking the earth again and again. It took her a moment to realize it was a horse running. Turning quickly, she saw a blur of black riding down the lane that led from the old barn.

"Hey!" she called out. "What are you doing?"

She felt her panic build as the rider stopped. The horse wheeled and reared, front legs pawing the air. The silver blade of a sword was caught just as the moon slipped out of the clouds. As the horse stood huge on its hind legs, the black-clad rider gave a long, low laugh.

As soon as the horse's feet touched the ground, the horse and rider galloped down the drive straight toward the bluffs. In the darkness, it seemed as if they disappeared over the edge.

Aurelia ran back toward the cottage, more determined than ever to sell the estate and get out of Natchez. Whether ghost or human, the intruder at Blackthorn spelled only trouble.

Chapter Two

"Once you pay the taxes you owe, you'll be left with close to half a million," Leon said as he refilled her wineglass. "How does that sound?"

Aurelia was watching the rain outside the restaurant window, which had undoubtedly washed away the horse tracks. Now she wouldn't be able to prove to anyone that the horse and rider were real flesh and blood, not some phantom or ghost. But who was riding on the estate, and why? She'd decided before Leon picked her up not to mention the incident to anyone until she had a chance to examine the grounds fully.

"Aurelia, did you hear my offer? I said you'd be left with half a million dollars, or thereabouts."

The words *half a million* finally pulled her attention from the mysterious horse and rider. "That's a lot of money," she said before she realized what she was saying.

"Yes, it is, and I'm glad you realize that," Leon

said, smiling. "I'll tell you what, we'll even keep the Blackthorn name. What about that?"

"What are you planning on doing with the estate?" Aurelia asked.

"The most unique shopping experience in the Southeast. Sort of an antebellum theme. Blackthorn Estate Mall. We could even incorporate Diable into the idea. How about a brew pub called Diable? That does have a ring to it, doesn't it? The finest microbrewery in Mississippi. I foresee a trip to Blackthorn Estate Mall as an experience akin to Disney World for the avid shopper."

Aurelia wasn't expecting the pang of grief that hit as she graphically visualized Leon's development dream. It wasn't a dream, it was more like a nightmare.

"I think if you bought the property, I'd have to ask you not to use anything related to Blackthorn. Once the estate leaves the family, I think it would be best for you to start over fresh."

Leon nodded. "I see your point. Actually, our first idea was to call it Riverbend. We were planning on putting a restaurant on the bluff, sort of Malibu construction hanging off the edge of that big bluff. Then there would be a walkway down the bluff to the river, where we would have our casino boat docked."

"You've thought of everything," Aurelia said dully.

"Yes, we have. That's why we're willing to pay such a handsome price for Blackthorn. If you'll just agree to sell, we can get the paperwork started tomorrow, and you'll have your cash by the end of the week.''

"Wow." It was everything Aurelia had hoped for, so why did she feel so bereft?

"Shall I schedule an appointment to sign the papers? I know the title folks, and we can rush the appraisal tomorrow morning.''

Aurelia leaned back in her chair. "This sounds wonderful, Leon, but I don't want to rush into anything this fast. I'd like to have the property appraised and then I'd like to give others a chance to make an offer on it. I understand there're some significant historical sites there, including an Indian burial ground. Perhaps a historical society would be interested in preserving the property.''

"They might be interested, but there won't be any funds. The entire state is in proration. There's no money for the necessities much less luxuries like historical preservation.''

Leon's tone rubbed Aurelia the wrong way. "Then perhaps a private citizen.''

"Like Marcus McNeese," Leon said, laughing. "He doesn't have two dimes to rub together. Television repair isn't exactly a gold mine.''

"How did you know Mr. McNeese came to see me about the property?'' Aurelia asked.

"I didn't know, but it was a damn good guess. He's been mooning around over that property since he was a teenager. He used to go up there and study the land, making little notes and drawing maps. He even tried to get the state to buy it several times for a park or landmark or something. There's never been any money for that.''

Aurelia felt her hopes drop. In the back of her mind, she'd grasped onto Marcus's suggestion that she sell the land to a historical group. And she'd hoped that Marcus would be able to put her in touch with such a group.

''Still, I'd like to give it a try. And I'd like a few days to walk the grounds. Blackthorn is my heritage, and I'd like to know it before I sell it.''

Leon leaned back in his chair and sipped his wine. ''Of course, if you don't accept my offer now, I'm not bound to it. I can lower the price.''

Panic gripped Aurelia. She couldn't afford to lose money to indulge her curiosity and Marcus McNeese's passion for preservation. She was about to accept Leon's offer when she felt a twinge of anger. Leon was trying to arm-wrestle her into a deal. Whether it was smart businesswise or not, she hated to be pushed and shoved. ''I guess I'll have to take that risk,'' she said. ''On the other hand, I might get a much better offer.''

She put her napkin on the table. It was pouring rain outside, and chances were the road that led up to her cottage would be slick and dangerous. She needed to get home before the road conditions got any worse. ''I'd like to go home now,'' she said.

Home. It wasn't a word she'd expected to use in reference to Blackthorn, but somehow it seemed right.

MARCUS MCNEESE SAT behind the wheel of the old pickup and watched Aurelia and Leon drive away from Madeline's. He had to hand it to Leon—he'd moved in fast for the kill. Marcus started the pickup and followed behind the Mercedes SUV. Once Aurelia was home, he wanted to try to talk to her again, before she signed any kind of deal with Leon. If she'd just give him a little time, he might be able to find a buyer for Blackthorn who would value the property as he did.

He would beg for that time if he had to, but he had something better, a possible solution.

The private lane that led to Blackthorn was treacherous when it was wet, and Marcus wondered if Leon had the skill to drive up it. Leon had many talents, especially in a courtroom where he excelled in eviscerating witnesses who gave testimony damaging to his clients. His ability behind the wheel of a vehicle was unknown.

When Leon turned to go up the private lane, Marcus drove past and stopped on the side of the highway. He'd wait until Leon came back down before he attempted to talk to Aurelia. This time, he'd done a little homework. Using a few contacts he still had in law enforcement, he'd learned that Aurelia's mother suffered from Alzheimer's disease and had been institutionalized for the past two years. Until that time, Aurelia had cared for Ursula Agee at home. Aurelia had given up her college education and her life. A point in his favor was Aurelia's field of study—she'd been a student of history. If only he could appeal to her love of the past, he might be able to persuade her to wait on selling Blackthorn. On the other hand, he knew how pressing her needs were. The facility her mother lived in ran a good three thousand dollars a month.

Now that he was more aware of her circumstances, he'd come up with a plan. He was willing to pay the nursing home costs for three months if Aurelia would give him that amount of time to come up with a buyer for Blackthorn. If he didn't find a buyer, Aurelia wouldn't be out anything.

If he could just present the idea to her in a way that didn't set her off, he might have a chance. She was a mite touchy in the temper department, but he understood now the responsibility that had been dumped on her since she was a teenager. Hardship often made people irritable. He knew that from experience. He'd gone through a period in his own life when almost any comment set him off.

As he sat in the dark, the rain beating down on the roof of the truck, he thought again of his first sighting of Aurelia. One reason he'd been so clumsy in his attempt to talk to her had been because of her beauty. He'd simply not anticipated that the heiress of Blackthorn could be a woman so lovely—and so unaware of her loveliness. She'd gotten annoyed with him because he was almost speechless. A lot of other women would have sensed the power it gave them and enjoyed it.

He was grinning at the memory when the SUV came back down the driveway. At least Aurelia hadn't lingered in saying her goodbyes to Leon. Marcus shook his head at the thought—was it possible he was just a little jealous? No, it was more that he wanted to protect Blackthorn, and Aurelia, from the likes of Leon. If Aurelia wasn't careful, she'd be holding a bag of beans instead of the title to Blackthorn. Leon was a slick manipulator, and he always got what he went after. Or almost always. This was going to be the exception.

AURELIA UNHOOKED her bra and slipped into the long flannel nightgown. Not exactly the stuff of TV commercials, but the gown was warm and the cottage was cold. She'd been afraid to leave the space heaters on while she wasn't inside. Though she had the gas jets turned up as high as they would go, it would take some time to heat the cottage.

She went to the window and stared out through the rain. Had she really seen a man on horseback? It would be easier to believe she'd imagined it. All those foolish stories! Perhaps she *had* let her imagination get away with her. She remembered the way the horseman had ridden into the night, disappearing at the edge of the bluff as if he'd been swallowed by the darkness or fallen into the river below. It couldn't have happened that way. If she wasn't careful, she'd be making up tales about a ghostly rider on a huge black horse.

Despite the eerie visit by the horseman, she had a substantial offer on Blackthorn. Even if no one else made a bid, she could sell the estate, pay the back taxes and realize a profit of almost a half million dollars. Properly invested, that would offer her mother comfort for the rest of her life.

At the thought of her mother she felt tears well in her eyes. It was so unfair. Her mother was only fifty-four. A horrible disease had cut her off from her life. There were times Ursula Agee didn't even recognize her daughter. Those were the times that almost broke Aurelia's heart.

There were so many things Aurelia wanted to talk to her mother about. There was Blackthorn and all that was happening here, and there was the scholarship to study history at Brown that had been offered to her. Of course she couldn't take it. She couldn't leave her mother totally in the care of strangers. As it was, she could get by to see her and check on her every day in Minneapolis. Brown was out of the question, but it was an honor to have been offered the chance. Her mother would be so proud of her.

At the familiar ache in her throat, Aurelia walked away from the window. There was no point hurting for things that would never be. Still, it would be nice to have someone to share the joyful moments with.

She saw the lights of the vehicle pulling up to her

house, and she wondered if Leon was coming back to twist her arm a little more. The idea of it made her determined not to sell Blackthorn until she followed her gut instincts and had it appraised.

The truck wasn't Leon's, and the man who got out of it was taller than Leon. When the man stepped up on the porch and threw back the hood of his raincoat, Aurelia recognized Marcus McNeese. Her first reaction was pleasant surprise, quickly followed by annoyance. Marcus wasn't going to pressure her, either. She was tired of people trying to jockey her into one corner or another.

She opened the door, forgetting she was in her nightgown until she saw Marcus's gaze sweep down her. Embarrassment only made her angry. "What are you doing here?" she asked in a tone that held no friendliness.

Marcus smiled. "Sorry to disturb you, Miss Agee, but I'd like to talk to you. I have a proposal that won't make you any money, but you won't lose any either. And it'll give me a chance to find a proper buyer for Blackthorn."

When Aurelia realized that Marcus wasn't going to lecture her on selling the estate, she relaxed a little. "What kind of offer?" Although it was sheer foolishness, she would prefer selling the estate to someone who would preserve it rather than develop it. Maybe Marcus had a buyer.

"It's just a little complicated, but—"

"Come inside," she said, aware that it was bitter

cold and wet outside, and that all of the heat was escaping from the cottage as she held the door open.

She didn't wait for him to respond. She walked into the bathroom and found her robe. When she came back he was standing in front of the space heater.

"My grandmother had a heater just like this," he said easily. "When I was a little boy, I'd warm my pants in front of it before I put them on in the morning."

"What kind of proposal did you have in mind?" Aurelia asked. Standing barefoot, she was more aware of Marcus's height and masculine build. Again, she noticed that he seemed more a man who labored physically than in a shop.

"I'd like to pay your bills and expenses for three months. In that time, you can seek buyers for Blackthorn and I'll try to find a historical group interested in purchasing it. If at the end of three months I haven't found a buyer, you can sell to whomever you wish. You won't have lost any money in the process."

Aurelia took in his offer. It was extremely generous and to her advantage. "I'd love to take you up on the offer," she said, "but there's a problem."

"What?" Marcus said.

"It isn't just my expenses. I have medical bills. They're high."

Marcus stared directly into her eyes. "I was sorry to learn about your mother, Aurelia. I wasn't prying, but I had to have the facts straight or I couldn't make this offer. I was including your mother's expenses in the proposal.''

''You were?'' Aurelia was stunned. ''That's very generous, Marcus. Very generous.''

''Then you'll accept my proposal?''

''There's something else.'' She bit her bottom lip in regret. ''The back taxes. I owe close to twenty thousand, and they're due in a month or the estate will be sold on the courthouse steps.''

''Oh,'' Marcus said softly, and she saw the defeat in his face. ''I can't come up with that kind of money, but I can help you file for a delay on the taxes. I'll do that tomorrow. We can buy a little time.''

''You really want to save Blackthorn, and not just for yourself,'' she said, realizing for the first time how much Marcus must care for the estate. ''Why?''

Marcus shifted his weight from one leg to the other. ''It's a long story.''

Aurelia indicated one of two chairs in front of the heater. ''Sit down, I'd like to hear your reasons.'' To her surprise, she found that she really did want to hear his reasons.

Marcus took the seat, then leaned forward and rested his elbows on his knees, his hands dangling. ''I grew up in Natchez. Sixth generation.'' He smiled self-consciously. ''I love this area, and I love the history. I grew up on stories of Andre Agee and Diable, his horse.'' He hesitated, looking at her.

''Yes, the Fantôme and his devil horse. I've heard all about him. In fact—'' Aurelia stopped herself just in time before she blurted out her earlier encounter with the ghostly horse and rider. She wasn't ready to admit to anyone that Andre had already paid her a visit.

"Yes?" Marcus pressed her.

"Oh, nothing. I've heard all the stories. Leon was quick to tell me all about the wicked Andre and his ghost."

"I don't believe Andre was wicked," Marcus said flatly. "I think he was hung for a lot of reasons, but being a highwayman wasn't one of them."

Aurelia got up and went to the cabinet under the kitchen sink. She'd been rummaging around earlier and found an unopened bottle of bourbon. She got two glasses out of the cupboard and washed them before she made two drinks. "Sorry, no ice and nothing except water for mixer." She handed one to Marcus. "Now tell me why you don't believe my ancestor deserved to hang. This is a story I'd really like to hear."

Marcus sighed and his shoulders relaxed. "Andre Agee was a man ahead of his time. He freed his slaves before the War Between the States, and he let them work for shares. They didn't get rich, but they were free men. He was well liked by both races. He was a highly respected man."

"Except for his little habit of stopping people on the Natchez Trace and robbing them." Aurelia sipped the bourbon. It wasn't her favorite drink, but with the cold, rainy night and the heater blazing, it was perfect.

"If you look at a list of the people Andre robbed,

it was mostly carpetbaggers and those who stole their riches in the first place."

Aurelia arched her eyebrows. "So, you'd like me to believe he was a Civil War era Robin Hood."

"Exactly," Marcus said, nodding. "I know it sounds like I've cooked up a tale to entertain you, but Andre Agee stole only from people who had come into ill-gotten gains. And he never kept any of the riches he stole."

"Really?" Aurelia loved the idea of the story, but she didn't believe it any more than she believed in ghosts.

"It's the truth, Aurelia. The carpetbaggers got together and hanged him. He was never given a trial or even a public hearing. A mob ambushed him and hung him right on this very estate."

The way Marcus told the story made it easy for Aurelia to visualize. "That must have been horrible."

"They hung him with his wife and children watching."

The gruesome image lingered in her mind even after she tried to dislodge it. "How awful."

"It was. I don't know how much you know about history," he said, pausing again, "but the South was invaded by the worst type of scum after the war. Reconstruction brought men who had no problem bleeding a land that was already ravaged and devastated. Your great-great-great-grandfather was a force of justice in a world that offered none to most Mississippians. He was loved by the majority of the people around here. It was only the parasites who hated him and eventually killed him.''

Aurelia had studied the war and the period of reconstruction that followed. She was well aware of the era of the carpetbaggers—men who came to the South to grow fat and rich on the suffering of others. What Marcus said could possibly be true, but it could also be a total fabrication.

''It's an interesting story,'' she said, ''but why are you so...invested in it?''

''I guess I just have a love of history, especially local history. I'd like to set the record straight on Andre Agee. He's been vilified for over a century and a half. He deserves better treatment.''

Aurelia couldn't help the smile that lifted the corners of her mouth. ''That's very noble of you, but it still doesn't tell me why.''

''For a long time I believed I could make a difference in the world. That I could help bring justice. Now I know that isn't true. The past is a lot safer to tamper with than the present.''

Marcus stood up. ''I've taken enough of your time, Aurelia.''

She followed him to the door, surprisingly reluctant to see him go. ''Thanks for telling me the story of Andre,'' she said, touching his sleeve. ''It was kind of you.'' And she realized then that Marcus McNeese was a kind man, a rarity in her experience.

''Good luck, Aurelia,'' he said, pulling the hood of his jacket over his head before he stepped into the rain.

Chapter Three

The wind blowing off the river was freezing, and Aurelia pulled her heavy jacket higher. Even with the polar-fleece lining, the coat wasn't warm enough. And people said Minnesota was cold!

The sun had just risen above the tree line, and Aurelia couldn't suppress the small gasp that escaped her at the beauty of the land and river that spread before her. Blackthorn was a beautiful place.

She waited until the sun climbed higher into the sky before she began hunting for any tracks that might remain from her nocturnal equestrian. He had to be real. She remembered the pounding of the horse's hooves, felt again the sensation of the earth shaking. Horse and rider were flesh. What she had seen had been no phantom.

But the rain had come down so hard the night before, there wasn't a trace of evidence remaining. As she stood on the edge of the bluff, she knew they hadn't somehow managed to ride down the bluff to the river. It was a sheer drop. So where had they gone, if they were flesh and blood? Goose bumps danced along her skin and it wasn't from the cold.

Turning away from the river, she started down the path that led to the old estate. In the dawn light, the pillars seemed to glow with a pinkish fire. There was something compelling about the place, she had to admit. In her mind she visualized the scene of Andre Agee's hanging. If it was the way Marcus believed, a great injustice had been done to her ancestor. She could see the angry mob taking Andre, his hands tied behind his back, to some makeshift gallows. She stopped in front of a huge white oak tree. One of the limbs looked perfect for use as a gallows.

And what of the wife and children? Rachel had been the wife's name. The children were nameless in her knowledge of the family history. What had become of them after they'd witnessed such a horrible thing?

She was deep in thought as she stood in front of the tree, the pillars to the south of her. She was so lost in her own thoughts that at first she didn't recognize the neighing of a horse for what it was. When it finally dawned on her, she set off to the east to track down the sound. There was a horse on the premises—she simply had to find it.

She passed the pillars and was suddenly stopped by a thicket of slender trees that grew so closely together they seemed impenetrable. The trees were grayish-black, and wicked thorns grew all over their trunks.

It looked as if anyone who dared to brave the thicket would be torn to shreds by the thorns.

"Devil's walking stick," she said softly to herself. The name was truly applicable, and it went well with Diable and the Fantôme. Blackthorn had certainly lent itself to legends.

The horse's neigh came again from the east, and Aurelia began to run, skirting the thicket. She found herself on a path that led into the deepest woods she'd ever visited. These were the virgin trees that had withstood axe and plow, the endless quest by man to conquer and develop. Andre Agee, her forefather, had preserved these woods. She had no time to enjoy the scenery as she began to run toward the sound of the horse.

After what seemed an eternity, Aurelia broke out of the woods into a meadow of bright-green grass. In the dismal brown of February, the grass was a startling color. In the distance was a small barn. As Aurelia drew in a deep breath, she heard the horse's call again. It spurred her to new energy and she began to run harder.

Ducking under a barbless wire fence, she ran into the barn and stopped. Two horses were contained in stalls, and both turned to give her a curious look. One was a beautiful steel gray and the other a buckskin. Neither was the enormous black horse she'd seen the night before.

"Aurelia!" Marcus said as he stepped out of a

room with two buckets of grain in his hand. "What are you doing here?"

"I could ask you the same thing," she said, still slightly breathless.

"I'm feeding my horses," he said as he dumped the sweet feed into a manger for the gray. He walked over and fed the buckskin. "The big boy over there is Cogar, and this is Mariah."

"Am I still on the grounds of Blackthorn?" Aurelia asked.

"You are," Marcus said. "I've sort of leased this land for the past five years. Since there was no person living on the estate, I've done what I could to maintain some of the pastures as payment. I planted that field of rye out there." He gave a crooked smile. "There was no one to pay."

"And no legally binding lease," Aurelia pointed out.

"No, there is nothing binding. As soon as the property is sold, I'll move the horses."

Aurelia realized how ugly she'd sounded. "I'm sorry. That was uncalled for." She walked over to the gray and tentatively reached out her hand to rub his face. "Is he nice?"

"Most of the time," Marcus said. "He's been known to have his moments."

"I heard the horses calling and…" She broke off the sentence and looked at Marcus. She wanted to tell him about the horse and rider, but he'd either think she was nuts or try to convince her that she'd seen the ghostly Andre Agee on Diable. She didn't believe either was true.

"Is something wrong, Aurelia?" he asked.

She had to remember that he was an extremely perceptive man. "No, I just don't know much about horses. I don't really like them. They're so big."

"Why don't we go for a ride? Mariah will take good care of you. You can see a lot more of Blackthorn by horseback than you can on foot."

It was a wonderful suggestion, except Aurelia was afraid. "I've never ridden." She laughed self-consciously. "When I was five, I used to pretend that I was a cowgirl, but I never had a chance to ride a real horse."

"As soon as they finish their breakfast, you're going to have your chance."

"I don't know...." Aurelia said, the hesitation clear in her voice.

"I'll make you a promise. Mariah will take good care of you, and we won't leave a walk unless you want to go faster."

MARCUS GLANCED at Aurelia, taking pleasure in her obvious delight as they walked the horses through the woods. Many of the hardwoods were bare of leaves, but Aurelia had fallen in love with the huge magnolia trees with their large green leaves and bloom pods covered in red seeds.

"Wait until May, when they bloom," Marcus assured her. "Then you can close your eyes and inhale and you'll think you're in heaven.'' He saw her face fall and regretted his words.

''I won't be here in May,'' she said softly. ''I'm beginning to wish I could be, but it just isn't possible.''

It was the closest she'd come to admitting she could feel anything for the estate, and Marcus felt his hopes lift. If Aurelia wanted to keep Blackthorn, perhaps there was a way they could manage it.

''Are there any other horses on the property?'' Aurelia asked.

''No, why?'' Marcus watched the frown that drew her eyebrows together.

''Just curious.''

He knew it was more than that, but he didn't press the issue. ''This land once grew cotton, and there were cattle as well as horses. Blackthorn was once self-sufficient in producing meat and vegetables. Even after the war, Andre's freed slaves remained at Blackthorn to farm. The Agee family had plenty of food. While a lot of the South was starving, he had enough to share. And he did share.''

''How was the house burned?'' Aurelia asked. She found she loved hearing Marcus talk about Blackthorn. He was weaving a fascinating history for her, and whether it was truth or fiction, she was beginning to want to believe it.

''The men who killed Andre believed he had some treasure hidden in the house. That's actually why they killed him. When he refused to tell them where the treasure was, they thought seeing him on the gallows would break Rachel or the children. But if there was a treasure, none of them talked. So the men burned the house down, believing that the money was buried beneath the foundation of the house.''

''And was it?'' Aurelia asked.

''I don't believe there was a treasure. As I told you earlier, whatever money Andre stole in his disguise as a highwayman, he returned to the people it rightfully belonged to.''

''I'd like to believe that, but it's a little too noble for me to swallow,'' Aurelia said. ''My experience with the Agee men is that they run off and leave their wives and children penniless.''

Marcus gave her a keen look. She did want to believe it, but life had taught her not to trust in nobility or such gestures. ''I believe it. I've studied all of the material available on Andre. His biggest mistake was in telling the people he robbed that they were thieves and robbers. He had a habit of publicly humiliating the very men he robbed. Working alone, he was an easy target. Once the rascals figured out it was Andre who was playing the masked highwayman, they greedily assumed he was keeping the wealth he stole for himself. They never believed he gave it away.''

''And did he actually give it all away?'' Aurelia asked.

''I've gone over his old accounts, which are in the public library here. They somehow escaped the fire.

He had no great source of income other than what he earned from the land.''

''If he was a thief, would he have kept accounts?''

''Why not? There wasn't an IRS back then,'' Marcus said with a touch of humor. ''Besides, I know for a fact he gave the money away.'' He caught her eye and held it. ''My family benefited from his generosity. Enough doubting now, I have great faith in one thing.''

''What's that?'' Aurelia asked.

''That you can gallop on Mariah.''

He didn't give her a chance to doubt herself. He urged Cogar forward knowing that Mariah would follow. When he glanced over his shoulder, he saw the rush of delight and pleasure on Aurelia's face as the mare's black mane whipped in her face. He'd been right about her, in more ways than one.

IT TOOK AURELIA only twenty minutes to bathe and change her clothes while Marcus waited on her.

''Hurry up, I'm starving,'' Marcus called as she twisted her dark curls up in a makeshift bun.

She came out of the bathroom reaching for her coat. ''I'm ready, and I'm starving, too. Does riding always make a person so hungry?''

She caught a hint of hunger in Marcus's eyes that had nothing to do with food. Instead of looking away, she was transfixed by Marcus's gaze and the way it made her feel—as if she couldn't catch her breath. She inhaled sharply and looked away, heat rising to her cheeks. In a split second, she'd had the most extraordinary fantasy. She'd been naked in Marcus's arms, the bedsheets tangled around their coupled bodies.

"Are you ready?" Marcus asked.

"Yes," she managed to reply, still flushed from her own imagination. She stepped outside, hoping the chill air would temper her flush.

Instead of one of Natchez's elegant restaurants, Marcus drove to an old diner. The parking lot was half-full of pickups and older cars. The neon sign flashed Ella's Diner.

"Ella is a friend of mine," Marcus said. "My shop is right there." He pointed to a large block building with a half dozen cars in front.

"Shouldn't you be at work?" Aurelia asked. In the pleasure of Marcus's company and the joy of her first horseback ride, she'd forgotten that there was a workaday world.

"Dan, my partner, has the shop going fine. He's technically a better repairman than I am." He shrugged. "He could manage without me."

Aurelia followed him in through the glass door and took a seat beside him at the counter. There were nearly two dozen patrons eating, and they all looked up and either smiled or called a greeting to Marcus. A couple of men at a far table gave catcalls and whistled.

The older woman who came up to the counter with a coffeepot in one hand and two cups in the other didn't bother to hide the fact that she was giving Aurelia the once-over.

"Who's this?" the woman asked Marcus bluntly.

"Aurelia Agee, this is Ella Jenson." Marcus smoothly made the introductions.

The earlier stare was nothing compared to the one Ella gave Aurelia on learning her name. "So this is the heiress of Blackthorn," Ella said loudly enough to stop the chatter in the diner. "You're as beautiful as Rachel. In fact, you look a great deal like her."

Aurelia recognized her great-great-great-grandmother's name, but she'd never seen a likeness of her. "How do you know?" she asked.

"You haven't been to the library?" Ella's penciled eyebrows shot up. "Heck, your family donated the money to start the original library. There's a portrait of Rachel and there was one of Andre, until our wise city voted to remove it since he was hung as a highwayman." She snorted. "A highwayman is a noble profession compared to the scoundrels who steal our hard-earned money in the guise of taxes and then squander it for personal gain."

Aurelia smiled. She liked Ella. The woman left no doubts where she stood on any issue. "I gather you're a fan of Andre, too," she said.

"Indeed I am. It was Andre Agee who brought the money to my great-great-grandmother to pay the taxes on her land so the carpetbaggers couldn't buy her out. Mr. Andre gave her enough money so that she could hang on until her cotton crop came through.

Over the years, the family sold off most of the land, but I still have the family house, and that's thanks directly to Andre.''

Aurelia felt Marcus's gaze on her and she ignored it. He'd brought her to the diner to hear this story. She was beginning to learn that he was a man who acted on his passions, and saving Blackthorn was definitely one of his passions.

''What do you know about the treasure Andre had hidden?'' Aurelia asked as she sipped her black coffee.

To her surprise, Ella's kind face drew into a frown. ''Not too loud about that, my dear. There are those who believe the treasure is still hidden on Blackthorn property. Half the kids who go up there are making out, but the other half are hunting for the treasure.''

Aurelia didn't bother to hide her amusement. ''If there was such a treasure, I'm sure over the last 150-odd years, someone would have found it.''

''Marcus and I both believe that Andre gave away all of the riches he stole. That was his way of handing out justice. He only gave the wealth back to the rightful owners. Like my family. The Jensons were never wealthy. Blacksmiths by trade. But there was a livery stable and a forge, and Benjamin Jenson was a fine craftsman. If you take a tour of the big mansions hereabouts, you'll see the wrought-iron work he did. He made a good living for his family until Reconstruction. His stable and forge were taken from him and he had no way to make a living except to farm the land. Had it not been for Andre, we would have been turned out and most likely starved.''

''I'm beginning to see Andre in a new light,'' Aurelia said, deliberately injecting a light tone into the conversation. Ella took her history seriously.

''How about some eggs, bacon, grits and toast?'' Marcus said, changing the subject. ''We're starving.'' He went on to tell Ella briefly of their ride.

''So you're learning the estate?'' Ella said as she wrote up the order. ''It's a lovely place, Aurelia. It means a lot to a good many folks around here. Even with all the heartache and tragedies, Blackthorn holds a special place.''

With that she was gone, checking on her customers.

''She's very nice,'' Aurelia said.

''She's got the biggest heart in Natchez. A hungry man has never been turned away from this diner. Anything left over she takes to the local shelter.''

''Ella said 'tragedies,' as in plural. What did she mean?'' Aurelia caught the sudden caution that flickered in Marcus's eyes.

''The estate has been abandoned for a long time. Folks have gone up there and camped. During the sixties and seventies, some hippies tried to start a commune up there. Things happened.'' He shrugged. ''A baby was left up there and abandoned. It died of exposure.''

''That's terrible,'' Aurelia said, a shiver moving up her spine. ''Who would do such an awful thing?''

''Young girls get desperate.'' He shook his head.

"Let's talk about something else. Did you know Andre adopted a child who was abandoned at Blackthorn?"

Aurelia laughed. "Andre was just a paragon of virtue, wasn't he? Next thing I know you'll be erecting a monument to him in downtown Natchez."

Ella set their breakfast down in front of them and refilled their coffee cups. "He was that," she said. "Some folks would try and make you believe differently, but don't listen to them. After the breakfast rush is over, about ten o'clock, you come around here and I'll tell you the real story of Andre Agee."

Chapter Four

Yvonne Harris was exactly what Aurelia expected from the two brief phone conversations she'd had with the Realtor. In one five-minute call she'd hired an enthusiastic Yvonne, and in another two-minute call, the terrified Realtor had quit.

"Miss Agee," Yvonne said, walking around her desk in three-inch stilettos to shake Aurelia's hand. "I'm so sorry things didn't work out between us. Is there something I can do for you now?" She gave Marcus a curious look.

"Mr. McNeese is helping me," Aurelia said. "I'd like to get Blackthorn appraised, and I'd like to know if you have a list of state agencies interested in historic properties. That would be my preferred buyer."

"I see." A calculating look crossed Yvonne's face. "Historic societies or the state may not be able to pay top dollar."

"I'd like to see what they offer," Aurelia said. "I don't have to take it."

"That's true." Yvonne picked up an organizer and began to flip the pages. "Our appraiser can get up to Blackthorn tomorrow morning, if that's convenient."

"Yes, that's fine."

"Be sure you're there," Yvonne said quickly. "I mean, after my experience no one wants to be up there alone." She made a face. "If you think I'm a coward, that's okay. I know that I've never been so terrified in my life."

"What exactly happened?" Marcus asked.

Yvonne gave him a disapproving glance, as if he had no right to participate in the conversation. "I'm sure you'll pooh-pooh my fears, Mr. McNeese. Everyone in town knows you've lusted after Blackthorn for years."

"I'd like to know what happened, too," Aurelia said smoothly. "If someone is making trouble on my property, I'll call the law to stop it."

"I don't think the sheriff will carry a lot of weight with a ghost," Yvonne said. "And that's what I heard. A ghost."

"What happened?" Aurelia pressed.

"I was in the woods." Yvonne sat against the edge of her desk, smoothing her carefully coiffed hair with her right hand. "I thought I could better represent the property if I knew more about it, and I hadn't seen the estate in a long time, since I was a teenager." She rolled her eyes on a laugh. "Anyway, I went into those woods. Magnificent, but very frightening. I was walking along, and I heard someone walking behind me."

"You're sure it was someone?" Marcus asked.

"I would take a step, and the person would take a step. When I stopped, they stopped."

"Did you see anyone?" Aurelia asked.

"I kept looking behind me, but no one was there. It was positively eerie."

"Could it have been a...well, an animal?" Aurelia was about to say *squirrel* but she didn't want to minimize the woman's obvious fear.

"No, it was something walking on two legs." Yvonne shivered. "But that's not the worst of it. I was frightened by someone following me, but then I heard *it*."

"Heard what?" Aurelia was being sucked into the story despite herself.

"I understand you're staying up at the cottage by yourself. Listen to me, Miss Agee, there isn't enough money in Natchez to get me to stay up there by myself."

"Did you hear a horse?" Aurelia asked.

"No." Yvonne's eyes were wide. "I've heard all the stories about Andre on his huge black horse. That's what I expected to hear. But this wasn't a horse." She leaned closer. "It was a baby crying. It was the saddest thing in the world. It sounded as if the poor infant was suffering terribly."

Marcus put his hand on Aurelia's arm. She was so startled she jumped.

"Sorry." He smiled at both women. "I just remembered, I have to get back to my shop. My biggest customer is coming by at eleven."

Aurelia nodded. "I'm ready. If you'd rather pass on this appraisal, Yvonne, I'll understand."

"I'm glad to help," the Realtor said, "just as long as I don't have to go back to Blackthorn, and from what I hear, this is going to be a quick sale. Everyone knows Leon has made an offer." She lifted her eyebrows, inviting more details.

"I'll be at the cottage tomorrow," Aurelia assured her. "Send the appraiser and we'll get this going. I can't stay in Natchez much longer."

"Yes, your mother is ill," Yvonne said.

Aurelia didn't bother to hide her surprise. "How did you know?"

"My dear, Natchez is a very small town. The heiress of Blackthorn is too delicious not to discuss."

Aurelia had never experienced public interest in her private business and she found it immensely distasteful. "I find that I'm too busy with my own affairs to meddle in other peoples'."

Instead of taking it as a reprimand, Yvonne only laughed. "You'll grow used to it," she said. "You'll even learn to enjoy it."

"I seriously doubt that," Aurelia replied as she walked to the door where Marcus waited.

"Andre Agee was loved by many and feared by more," Yvonne said. "As his heir, you got not only Blackthorn, but the burden of love, guilt and hate that comes with it. Your presence in town has stirred up a lot of old hatred and fear.''

AURELIA SAT QUIETLY on the drive back to Blackthorn, and Marcus knew she was digesting the things that Yvonne Harris had told her. Personally, he could have throttled the blond Realtor. All of that foolishness about a baby crying. It was just another story that had sprung up around Blackthorn because the estate had remained abandoned for so long.

"Yvonne is something of a pot stirrer," he said as he pulled up in front of the cottage.

Aurelia managed a smile. "Thanks for saying that. She has disturbed me a little, I guess."

"Any place left uninhabited is going to be grist for the spooky-story mill. What I don't understand is how Yvonne, no matter how frightened, would give up a commission. That's not like her at all. She'd evict her own mother if she could sell the property and make a dollar."

Aurelia laughed softly. "Isn't that a little harsh?"

"Perhaps," Marcus agreed, "but it made you smile."

"So a person's reputation is fodder for a smile from me?" She knew she was flirting and didn't want to stop.

"Your smile is worth a lot more than Yvonne Harris's reputation," Marcus said, and his hand brushed her cheek. Before he thought it through, his hand moved behind her hand and gently pulled her toward him. Aurelia gave no resistance, and when she was close enough, he kissed her.

It took only seconds for the kiss to go from exploratory to passionate. All other thoughts fled as Marcus felt Aurelia respond to him. When he finally broke the kiss, he sat back in his seat, eyes closed, and took a deep breath.

Looking over at Aurelia, he saw the flush on her cheeks and wondered if it was passion or embarrassment. He didn't have long to wonder.

"I don't know what came over me," Aurelia said quickly, her gaze on her knees. "I'm not in the habit of kissing men in parked cars."

She sounded so strained that Marcus didn't have the heart to tease her. Instead, he leaned over so that he could gently draw her face to his. His lips brushed hers softly, and when he felt her response, he drew back.

"You're a beautiful woman, Aurelia. I could kiss you all day and all night." He smiled at the surprise in her eyes. She was something of an innocent, and very proper, even in her thoughts. "But I have to go back to the shop. May I see you again tonight?"

He could see she was about to say no when he touched her lips with his finger. "Say yes," he whispered, holding her gaze with his.

"Yes," she said.

"At seven?"

"Perfect." She got out of the truck and walked into the cottage without a backward glance.

It was only as Marcus was pulling onto the highway that a flutter of worry for her safety touched him. He didn't put any stock into anything Yvonne Harris said. But what if there was someone else wandering around Blackthorn?

AURELIA LACED HER hiking boots and set off into the woods. The main path was clearly marked and wide enough for two horses to go abreast. As she walked she found the tracks the horses had made earlier that morning. A memory of the thrill of riding with Marcus flooded over her.

A side path veered to the right and Aurelia took it. In only a few moments, she felt as if she'd stepped into dusk. The tall trees grew so close together they seemed to absorb the sunlight. She'd been walking for about fifteen minutes when she heard something— or someone—rustling through the fallen leaves.

Instantly the incident related by Yvonne Harris came back to her. The Realtor had believed someone was stalking her. Aurelia began to walk faster, realizing with a jolt of horror that the person in the leaves had also increased his pace.

Trying to keep her fears in check, Aurelia began to run along the narrow path. A thin branch caught her cheek, drawing a cry of pain. Still running, she touched her fingers to her cheek and drew them back. There was blood on them.

Aurelia ran beside a huge oak tree and stopped when the path simply ended. She whirled around, seeking the source of the noise. Heart pounding, she realized the woods were completely quiet.

When the roaring of blood calmed in her ears, she realized the quiet was unnatural. Not even a bird fluttered or called. She looked around. The path that had been so clearly marked in the beginning was gone. In her panic, she must have strayed off it, and now she was lost in the big stretch of woods.

Taking a breath, she checked the sun. She'd been running to the east, so it was a simple matter of going back west. Eventually she'd come across the main path.

As she started walking forward, she listened for the sound of someone keeping pace. She heard nothing.

Nothing around her seemed familiar, and she knew there was no possibility that she might come across a landmark she would recognize. She could only keep walking in a westerly direction and hope that whatever had been following her was gone.

That thought brought another surge of panic, and she forced it back and kept walking calmly. Panic was what had gotten her into the mess she was in.

The trees seemed to crowd more closely together, and she veered to avoid a cluster of what looked like holly shrubs. The ground sloped to an old creek bed, and she grabbed at branches and roosts as she slipped down the bank. She was almost at the bottom when the leaves beneath her feet began to churn.

Startled, she fell backward, landing on her bottom in the slick leaves. Before she could stop herself, she was sliding down the bank. She landed in the churning leaves, screaming as a young man jumped out of the leaves and to his feet.

He started to run as she was scrambling up.

"Stop!" she yelled at him. To her complete shock, he did. As he turned slowly to face her, his head hung in shame.

"I'm sorry," he said. "They told me not to come back here, but I couldn't help it. I came to see Mariah, and then I just wanted to see my old home. I miss it here. And they said you were going to tear everything down and put in shops."

Listening to the young man's speech, Aurelia realized he was more a child than a grown man. "Who are you?" she asked, standing and brushing the leaves from her clothes.

"Joey Reynolds," he said, coming forward and helping to brush the leaves from her back. "I'm sorry I scared you. Then I tried to hide, but you were lost."

"Do you know how to get out of these woods?" Aurelia was over being angry and afraid. Now she was simply relieved.

"Sure. I lived here. This was where me and my mama stayed. Then she died and I had to go live in town."

"You lived in the cottage?" Aurelia asked.

"The place you're living now. That was where me and Mama lived."

"Show me how to get back there," Aurelia requested and was immensely relieved when Joey struck off in a westerly direction, talking to her over his shoulder as they went.

By the time they got to the cottage, she knew that Joey's father had been caretaker on the estate until fifteen years before, when he'd been killed in a car wreck. Lionel Agee, the absentee owner of Black-thorn, had allowed Joey and his mother to continue living on the estate until three years ago when Mrs. Reynolds had died. After his mother's death, Joey was moved into town where he lived in a small apartment owned by a local church.

"If you don't tear the cottage down, I could live here and take care of Blackthorn," Joey said as he paused on the front porch. "I don't like living in town. I love it here. I could stay and take care of everything."

Of all the appeals for Blackthorn, none had touched Aurelia's heart like Joey's. To him, the small cottage was home and it was where he had the best memories of his life with a family.

"Come in," she said, opening the door. "I'll make some hot chocolate."

Joey needed no urging. He went inside and began building a fire. When he was finished, he took a seat at the kitchen table, waiting patiently for Aurelia to make the chocolate.

"Joey, when you lived here did you ever hear or see a horse, other than Mariah and Cogar?" Aurelia put the cocoa down in front of Joey and then sat with her own cup in the other chair.

"Oh, sure. I saw Andre and Diable all the time."

He spoke with such casualness that Aurelia smiled. "So, you're not afraid of the highwayman and his devil horse?"

"Naw," Joey said, sipping the chocolate. "He's a nice man. He helped my mama's family a long time ago."

"How?" Aurelia asked.

"There was this man who came down here and tried to get the land. Andre caught him one night on the Natchez Trace and hung him up in a tree so that just his toes touched the ground. He told him to leave us alone or he would be sorry. When the man got cut down, he moved back to Boston." Joey grinned. "My mama said I should never be afraid of Andre. And Diable is beautiful."

"But," Aurelia was puzzled, "they're ghosts."

"Sure, but ghosts only hurt people who are afraid of them, and I'm not afraid. Why would I be afraid of Andre? I've never stolen anything in my life."

Aurelia sat back in her chair and let the warm mug of cocoa thaw her frozen fingers. Indeed, who would be afraid of a ghost?

"Joey, would you like a ride back to town?" she asked.

"No, ma'am. I'd rather stay here if it's okay with you."

For a split second Aurelia was tempted. She liked the young man and found him comforting. But it wasn't appropriate for him to share the tiny cabin with her.

"You can't stay here now," she said. But if she did sell Blackthorn, perhaps she could arrange it so that Joey had a place to stay as long as he lived. There was such a thing as a life estate, where a person could sell land but allow someone to live on it until his death. What would it hurt to keep one tiny little area safe for Joey?

"Are you going to make Marcus move Mariah and Cogar?" Joey asked.

"I haven't really thought all of this through," she said far more gently than she'd spoken of Blackthorn's future to anyone else.

"Those horses love it here. They're like me," Joey said. "We could be happy if people would just leave us alone."

Aurelia reached across the table and touched Joey's hand. "I know just what you mean," she said.

"Even Diable likes living here," Joey said.

"Diable? He lives here, too?" Aurelia asked.

"Of course. Where else would he live?" Joey looked up at her. "One day I'm going to catch him and ride him."

Aurelia finished her cocoa. "And what will Andre say about that?" she asked.

"Oh, he won't care. He only needs him at night, when he wants to frighten the folks who come out here."

"Oh, the teenagers who park on the property?" Aurelia asked.

"Yeah, them and the others. The ones who come out here digging for the treasure."

Aurelia was amused. "So, they still come hunting for Andre's stash, do they?"

"They do, but they won't find it. My mama said he hid it so no one will ever find it. But they all want it. They don't care about anything but the treasure." Joey's normally smiling face now held a frown. "They're all greedy. All of them. And one day Andre's going to catch them and make them sorry."

Aurelia picked up her jacket. "We'd better go, Joey."

"Can I come back? They said if I came up here I had to ask permission."

"Sure," Aurelia said. "You're welcome here until I sell the property. Just come by the cottage and let me know you're here, okay?"

"That's a deal," Joey said, holding out his hand for her to shake.

Chapter Five

Aurelia stopped the car in front of the church where Joey had a small apartment. She could see by the expression on his face that he'd rather be at Blackthorn, but it just wasn't possible. Not yet.

"It's okay, Joey," she said. "I'll be at Blackthorn for a few more days, at least. You can visit while I'm there."

"Okay," he said. She got out of the car and stood with him on the sidewalk. Her heart was heavy at the young man's unhappiness. Life simply wasn't fair.

"See you soon, Aurelia," he said, making an effort to smile. Aurelia watched him until he went inside. In a moment he returned to the doorway holding the stray cat he'd adopted. Aurelia waved, and he waved back. His expression was one of trust, and Amelia felt a jolt of guilt. Joey loved Blackthorn, and she was the one who was selling it, probably to someone who would destroy it. Joey would never understand her reasons.

She started toward her car, her attention caught by a stout woman in a navy coat. The woman was coming down the sidewalk toward her like a bulldog on a mission.

"Aurelia Agee!" the woman called.

Aurelia paused with her key in the door of the car. "Yes, can I help you?"

"You certainly can. You can head back up to Minnesota or wherever it was you came from. You have no business in Natchez or on Blackthorn land."

Aurelia took a deep breath. "Who are you?" she asked the woman with the blazing gray eyes.

"I'm Lottie Levert, and Blackthorn is mine."

The claim was so preposterous, Aurelia thought she'd misunderstood the woman. But one look at her clenched jaw, and Aurelia knew the woman meant business. "Do you have legal documentation?" Aurelia asked. Lottie Levert's claim was outrageous. Aurelia had the deed to Blackthorn in her possession. Her mother had inherited the estate upon the death last year of Lionel Agee.

"I don't need legal documents. Blackthorn is mine, by right. My great-great-grandmother was Andre Agee's daughter. She was born on the wrong side of the sheets, but she's his blood and Blackthorn should have passed to her and then to me. Me and my son, Randall, want what's ours. We thought we'd buy the place at the tax sale, but it seems you've arrived just in the nick. Well, my pretty lady, you won't get away with it."

Aurelia didn't know whether to laugh or call a lawyer. Lottie Levert was a woman with a lot of energy and a curious way of talking. "Have you got legal documentation of your claim?" Aurelia repeated.

"I've got the blood in my veins. I'm perfectly willing to spill a little of it and take a DNA test."

Aurelia frowned. "I'm not certain that's possible, and I don't think it matters. The estate was willed to my mother. I don't think blood or kinship has anything to do with it."

Lottie put her hands on her hips. "I figured that's what you'd say. I told Randall we'd have to fight this out with you. He wanted to talk to you all gentlemanly, but I told him it was best left woman to woman. I'm telling you square, you won't get Blackthorn from us."

"Blackthorn isn't mine. I'm acting as my mother's agent," Aurelia said, hoping to make the woman understand. "She's very ill, and the property must be sold."

"And I'm not in the best of health, but that won't prevent me and Randall from going to the mat on this. You're a fine and fair lady, as anyone can see, but a pretty face doesn't give you the license to come in here and steal from us Leverts!"

It was one thing for Lottie to lay claim to Blackthorn, but quite another to accuse Aurelia and her mother of theft. Anger made Aurelia's lips tighten. "I'm not stealing a thing. Blackthorn is mine. By legal will."

A cluster of men and women were walking down the sidewalk toward Aurelia. She had no desire to continue the conversation with the loud Lottie Levert in front of them.

"If you have anything else to say to me, please speak to my lawyer, Mr. Leon Kimball," Aurelia said.

"Ha!" Lottie yelled, rushing forward. "You won't talk to me but you'll let that scalawag Leon tend to your business. You're trying to cheat me out of my inheritance, and you're going to get skinned like a baby lamb at harvest time! You're playing a dangerous game here, my fine lady, and the cards are marked against you."

Aurelia glanced at the three women and two men who'd stopped in their tracks, mouths open, as Lottie Levert bellowed.

Aurelia put the key in the car door and pulled it open. When she did so, Lottie Levert threw up her hands, screamed, and fell over on the grass.

"She pushed me down!" Lottie cried. "That girl is stealing my inheritance and she's trying to kill me! She threatened to do worse if I didn't give up my claim to Blackthorn." She began to roll back and forth across the grass.

Aurelia froze. She was still standing with her hand on the car door when one of the women rushed forward and knelt beside Lottie. The others joined her and in a few moments they had Lottie calmed down and sitting up.

"You're all witnesses to the fact that the girl there threatened me and then tried to kill me," Lottie said, barely able to control the smile that tugged at her lips. "She's stealing my land and she's trying to put me six feet under."

"I saw no such thing, Lottie Levert," the first woman on the scene said. "I saw you throw yourself to the ground." The woman looked up at Aurelia and rolled her eyes. "You must be Aurelia Agee. I'm Marthe Lumpkin. I'm a friend of Marcus McNeese."

Aurelia felt instant relief. "I didn't touch her."

"I saw her fall," Marthe said, motioning the men to lift Lottie to her feet. "Everyone in town knows Lottie has been claiming Blackthorn as her own for the past twenty years."

"It is mine," Lottie said huffily. "You were born with a silver fork in your hand, Marthe. No point in you being uppity with me."

"You'd best be on your way, Lottie," Marthe said, not unkindly. "You've made enough of a scene today and I don't think Randall will like it. He's worked too hard to build his business here in Natchez for you to run all over town acting the fool."

"I'll be back," Lottie said as she looked at Aurelia. "This isn't over till the fat swan sings."

As she bustled off down the sidewalk, Aurelia was left standing among the group of people. "Thank you," she said to Marthe Lumpkin. "Would she really have gone to the sheriff and accused me of assaulting her?"

"If she thought she could get Blackthorn from you, she'd accuse you of flying on a broomstick." Marthe laughed at Aurelia's shock. "No one believes Lottie." She shrugged a shoulder. "It's hard to see it from your point of view, but Lottie isn't all bad. She's greedy and she has this fantasy about being the heiress of Blackthorn, but she also works with special children and does volunteer nursing in the VA hospital in Jackson."

"Is she really an illegitimate heir of Andre?"

"There's no telling about that one. Her great-great-grandmother never married, and it was said she worked at Blackthorn as a very young girl shortly before Andre was hanged. I suppose it could have happened."

Aurelia felt faintly dizzy. This was all she needed. Some kind of cousin laying claim to the property. "Why hasn't Lottie made a claim on Blackthorn before now?"

"Old Lionel wouldn't talk to her. He said she was crazy. The last ten years, he lived in London, too, so it wasn't easy to talk to him."

"He's been dead almost a year, and he didn't pay the taxes for a while before he died. She's had plenty of time to make a claim in the tax assessor's office."

"I suppose it never occurred to anyone that there was another branch of the family. A Yankee branch." Marthe smiled as she spoke. "Everyone in town knew the estate was going to be sold for taxes. There was quite a long list of folks believing they were going to buy the property for a song. Your appearance in Natchez has put a kink in some folks' plans.'' Marthe leaned closer. ''To that end, I'd be as careful as I could. Some folks still believe there's treasure buried at Blackthorn. This may be their last opportunity to suss it out.''

''Meaning I'm in the way?'' Aurelia didn't like the tingle of apprehension that came with the words.

''If someone were to find the treasure, they wouldn't want to share with you.'' She lifted her eyebrows. ''Get my drift?''

Aurelia nodded. ''Do you believe there's a treasure?''

''No treasure, no ghost,'' Marthe said, shaking her head. ''But if you could take an anonymous poll, I'll bet at least half the citizens of Natchez believe in the treasure and in Andre Agee's ghost.''

''How interesting,'' Aurelia said.

''Be careful, and if you hear anything unusual on the grounds, be smart and stay inside. Call the police. Sheriff Colson is a pretty decent guy. And he's not inclined to put up with a lot of foolishness.''

''Thanks,'' Aurelia said as she slipped into the car. As she drove away she watched Marthe rejoin her group. They were chatting and laughing, and suddenly, Aurelia had never felt so much alone.

MARCUS SCREWED the back of a television set into place and shook his head. ''Here you go, Mrs. Moss. I'll carry it out to the car for you.''

"How much is it, Marcus?"

"No charge," he said, glad his partner, Dan, was out back smoking a cigarette. Dan was always telling Marcus he did too many free repairs. But Mrs. Moss was on a pension, and her television was her only companion. He was glad to repair it for her.

Once he stowed the set in the back seat and made sure she was going to have help getting it inside her house, he started back inside the shop.

"That Lottie Levert made another scene today," Mrs. Moss said. "She tried to make out that the new heiress of Blackthorn pushed her down."

Marcus stopped and slowly turned around. "What?"

"Lottie made it a point to tell Aurelia Agee that cock-and-bull story that she's the illegitimate heir of Blackthorn and the rightful owner of the property."

"What a load—"

"Exactly!" Mrs. Moss said. "But she repeats it everywhere. There should be a law." She gave Marcus a wicked look. "Perhaps there is one. If you'd only take up your practice again, Marcus—"

"I'm done with the law," Marcus said. Realizing he might have spoken more harshly than he intended, he added, "And who would repair your television if I went back to the law?"

"You're a better lawyer than you are television repairman," Mrs. Moss said with a sniff. "Folks around here who wanted someone honest and fair knew they could count on you to look out for their legal interests. You try on the televisions, Marcus, but everyone in town knows Dan does all the difficult repairs. Go back to the law.''

Marcus shook his head. ''That's the past.''

''It wasn't your fault that young man went to prison. You did everything you could have done. The physical evidence was against him, and there was an eyewitness.''

''An eyewitness who was wrong,'' Marcus said, unable to keep the bitterness out of his voice. ''Wade Gammit died in prison for a crime he didn't commit.''

''What could you have done differently?'' Mrs. Moss asked.

''Another lawyer might have been able—''

''Hogwash!'' She straightened her back. ''Standing in the street like this isn't the place for this discussion, but just let me say that you've punished yourself enough for a crime you never committed. If you're so all-fired upset about a miscarriage of justice, take a look at how you've misjudged yourself.''

She walked around the car, got in behind the wheel and drove away without another word.

Marcus stood on the sidewalk until she'd disappeared. Mrs. Moss had been a friend of his grandmother's. She'd known him since he was a young man, when he'd mowed her grass for four dollars. She was overly fond of him and prejudiced. But no matter what she said, he couldn't forgive himself for failing a client.

He was done with the law, and that was that.

Walking back inside his shop, he thought about what Mrs. Moss had said about Lottie Levert. The woman was a menace to society. She did a number of good deeds, but she was always stirring up trouble somewhere. Her son, Randall, ran a used car lot on the south side of town and was apparently a good businessman. The business had grown from a dozen cars to one of the largest used dealerships in the state.

Marcus began putting away his tools as he thought about the Leverts. As far as he knew, Randall had never made any claims to being the heir of Blackthorn, though Lottie harped on it constantly. Perhaps he should stop off at the car lot and have a little talk with Randall.

"Will you lock up?" he called to Dan.

"Sure thing, Marcus. See you tomorrow."

Marcus got in his truck and drove through the old city of Natchez. The town had suffered a lot of damage during the War Between the States, but nothing like Vicksburg, just upriver. While Vicksburg had been bombed and starved into near total destruction, many of the old Natchez mansions still flourished.

Marcus drove past the entrance to Killburn, one of the loveliest old homes, where the first of the season's Mardi Gras balls would be held the next evening. The invitation list was exclusive, and no guest was allowed without a mask. Marcus found the party rather silly, but he did enjoy the beauty of the event.

At the car lot he got out, taking in the endless rows of gleaming vehicles. Randall's business was thriving.

When he went into the office, he learned that Randall was out of town for several days.

"Would you care to leave a message?" the pretty receptionist asked, giving Marcus a warm smile.

"I'll catch up with him later," Marcus told her.

He had a few hours to kill until it was time to pick up Aurelia. He decided to go up and check on the horses. The bitter weather was like a tonic to them, but Marcus knew how delicate a horse could be. It was safest to check on them, and it would give him a chance to lounge Diable.

AURELIA HELD THE heavy cream envelope in her hand and wondered who had left an invitation tucked inside the screened door of her cottage.

The flap was sealed with a blob of vermilion wax with an imprint of a jester in it. There was no return address.

Using her thumb, she broke the seal and opened the letter. Scanning the contents, she let out an excited gasp. She was invited to a masked ball at Killburn Estate. Masks were required.

Aurelia held the invitation to her chest. Since coming to Natchez she'd felt just a little like some fairy-tale figure. Now a masked ball! It was like something on a television movie.

There was no name on the invitation, but there was a handwritten note. "Please forgive the last-minute nature of the invitation. There's a wonderful dress shop on Magazine Street."

Aurelia bit her bottom lip. She was going to a ball! And she'd made up her mind, she was going to go. Most of her life had been spent doing things she ought to do. This time she was going to do something she wanted to do, no matter that it was last minute and a little insane. How many balls would she be invited to in Minneapolis? The answer to that was none.

This trip to Natchez had brought horseback riding and balls into her life. It would at least give her memories to take back with her when she had to return to Minnesota and her mother.

Speaking of her mother, she went to the telephone to call the hospital and check on her mother's condition. To her surprise, the line was dead. She depressed the switch-hook several times and checked the line on the old-fashioned phone. That was something she needed to do when she got into town, buy a new phone. But the phone had been working perfectly the day before. It was likely the lines were down. When Marcus came, she'd ask him to report it in the morning.

At the thought of Marcus, her heart began to beat furiously. He'd actually kissed her. And she'd kissed him back. Like a teenager. She looked in the bathroom mirror. How would she know how a teenager would act? She'd never been one. Maybe chronologically, but certainly not in any other aspect.

So it was okay to feel a tingle of excitement at the idea that she'd see Marcus again. It was okay to delight in the idea of buying her first ball gown. It was perfectly fine to anticipate dressing up with a mask and spending an evening among Natchez society.

She went back to the kitchen and put on the kettle for a cup of tea. Whoever would have thought she'd be living on a haunted estate? Life sure had thrown her a few kinks and curves.

She was just pouring water for the tea when she heard the faint sound of a baby crying.

Opening the door, she stepped outside and listened. The sound was erratic and she couldn't tell where it was coming from. She could feel her pulse rate increase, but this time it wasn't from pleasant anticipation.

Leaving the cottage door open, she walked down the drive. The crying seemed to be coming from the woods, but she couldn't be certain.

Dusk was falling and she lingered near the cottage. Truth be told, she was getting a little spooked by Blackthorn. So many things had happened on the property. Aside from Andre, there was the crying baby that Yvonne had said she'd heard. But she hadn't put any credence in Yvonne's story, or any of the stories. Maybe she should have.

The crying stopped as suddenly as it started. Aurelia was some fifty yards down the driveway shivering in the cold. She listened again, and when she heard nothing, she ran back to the cottage. As she closed the door, she leaned against it. Of the ghosts at Blackthorn, she definitely preferred Andre and his horse.

Chapter Six

The drive up to Blackthorn Estate's caretaker's cottage was newly graveled, but Marcus drove slowly. The undergrowth had also grown too close to the road and at times brushed against his truck. The drive needed to be trimmed back, and that was the least of it. The once lush fields were fallow, the soil nourishing only scrub trees and brambles, except for the twenty acres Marcus maintained for his horses' use. Since Lionel Agee's death, no attempts had been made to maintain the estate.

In the past, it had been a glorious sight. He remembered picnics on the old estate when Lionel was still alive. The whole town would be invited to spread a blanket under the huge live oaks that covered at least forty acres around the house.

Lionel would hire a band, traditionally bluegrass, for the entertainment of the picnickers. It had been at such a spring gathering that Marcus's father, Tom, had proposed to his mother, Anna, or so he'd been told as a boy. His mother had been fond of family stories, especially love stories between her and Tom. The two of them had ignited the spark of romance in Marcus when he was just a child. They also fostered his love of heroes and heroic acts.

As he slowly made his way up the drive, he could almost hear his mother's voice. To hear her tell it, Andre Agee had been better than Robin Hood. He'd been justice, vengeance and financial retribution all in one swift slash of his sword. And as far as legend was concerned, Andre used his sword basically for show. There were no reports of his killing anyone, though he had left a few of Natchez's leading lights in humiliating situations. Such as the time Andre accosted the mayor of Natchez, a newly arrived carpetbagger who'd illegally taken the old mayor's home, store and position. Andre had captured the old scalawag on the Natchez Trace, taken every penny he had on him and left him, pants around his ankles, tied to a tree.

The stories still made Marcus grin. When he was almost at the cottage, he saw where a limb had fallen, pulling the telephone wires down. Luckily, the power lines still seemed to be in place.

When Aurelia opened the door to his knock, he felt again the sensation of being breathless. She was wearing a red sweater-dress that clung to her slim body.

"You look stunning," he said, aware that he was staring and unable to stop himself. At last he met her gaze and realized she was blushing. "You're a very beautiful woman,'' he said, and when her blush deepened, he added, ''Red is definitely your color.''

''Thank you.'' She stepped back so he could enter, and when he was seated in a rocker in front of the fire, she handed him a drink. ''I forgot to buy liquor in town. It was quite an eventful day, but I did fill the ice trays.''

''The drink of bourbon and water is fine, and I heard a little about your day. Lottie Levert.'' He smiled at her surprised reaction.

''How did you know?''

''This is a small town. You've been the primary topic of discussion for a week now, and Lottie just added a little spice to the mix. You might even wind up in Miss Suzy's society gossip column in the *Natchez Ledger.*''

''My lifelong ambition is fulfilled. I'll thank her next time I see her,'' Aurelia said, sitting in the rocker beside Marcus. ''Lottie is an unusual woman.''

''That's a kind way of saying she's crazy as a loon,'' Marcus agreed. ''She is that. But her son seems like a reasonable man. Or at least the few times I had dealings with him he seemed sensible.'' He started to tell her that he'd dropped by the car lot, but he hesitated. Aurelia was an independent woman. She might not appreciate his help, and as it turned out, he hadn't been a help.

''What about her claim?''

''To Blackthorn?'' Marcus laughed. ''I'm afraid Lottie has some need to align herself with what she considers an upper-crust family. She's gone around all of her life claiming she's a descendant of Andre. Most folks find her pathetic, but she's basically harmless. Or so I thought. Mrs. Moss said there was some physical contact.''

''No, not really. She threw herself to the ground and then accused me of pushing her down. She also said I threatened her.'' Aurelia flushed again as she was talking. ''There were people on the sidewalk watching. I felt like a fool.''

Marcus put his drink down and reached over to take her hand. ''Lottie is the fool. You were merely an innocent victim.''

''Do you think she really believes she should have Blackthorn?''

In that question, Marcus heard Aurelia's doubts about her chosen course of action. He understood that no matter how crazy Lottie might be, Aurelia had no desire to cheat her or take from her what was her right.

''I don't believe a word of it. In fact, when Lionel was alive he got so tired of Lottie's constant whining that he offered to have a DNA test just to prove that she was no kin to him at all.''

''What happened?''

''Lottie refused, as everyone knew she would.''

''She was yelling that she would have a blood test. 'Spill her blood' was the exact phrasing she used.''

Marcus laughed. ''Easy to do now, since Lionel's dead. Even if he were alive, the test would actually show nothing except possibly some blood kinship—to you. There's technically no way to prove who Lottie's great-great-grandparents were.''

''But you don't believe her claim?''

Marcus squeezed her fingers. ''No, I don't.''

''How is it you know so much about DNA?'' Aurelia asked.

Marcus hesitated. He'd tried so hard to bury the past, what he once was, what he once had done. But as he'd frequently pointed out to Aurelia, Natchez was a very small town. Someone would eventually tell her.

''I was a lawyer once. In trying cases I learned a lot about DNA.''

He saw that his revelation had shocked her yet again. ''Why did you quit?''

Here it was. Truth time. ''A man I represented was innocent of the crime. He was convicted and sent to prison, where he was killed.''

The hand he held suddenly curled around his fingers and held him. ''I'm sorry,'' Aurelia said softly. ''That must have been hell for you.''

''I've tried to simply put it behind me, but I never wanted the responsibility of a man's life again. I enjoy working on the televisions. If I mess up,'' he smiled with one corner of his mouth, ''I can always buy my customer a new set. That doesn't bother them at all.''

Her gaze searched his face and he did his best to hide the pain that he couldn't manage to shake.

"This is going to sound horrible, but I'm going to tell you the truth." Aurelia's gaze held his, her eyes intense, and he suddenly saw the pain there, too. "Once my mother dies, I don't ever want to be responsible for anyone again. I worry constantly that she won't have the things she needs, that I won't be able to provide properly for her. I understand completely that you don't want that kind of burden."

Marcus saw the tears in her eyes and slipped from his chair to kneel beside her. He gathered both of her hands in his. "I never suspected you would understand. No one else in town does. They think I'm a little nuts."

Aurelia shook her head. "I do understand." She slid a hand free and put it against his cheek. "Now enough dark talk. I got a surprise today."

Marcus had never admired Aurelia more than he did as he watched her deliberately pull herself from the brink of sadness. She was quite a woman.

"What kind of surprise?" he asked, rising to his feet while still holding her hand.

"An invitation. To a ball."

"At Killburn Estate?"

"Are you going?" she asked, delight clear on her face.

"The guest list is a secret," Marcus said, smiling at her pleasure. "Only the cream of Natchez society is invited. I don't think a lowly television repairman qualifies."

As he watched her face fall he regretted his teasing.

Aurelia, for all of her iron will, was still naive. "But then again, you never know. I might be one of the masked men who ask you to dance."

"I certainly hope so," Aurelia said. "I have to buy a dress tomorrow. My very first ball gown. They don't have a lot of masked balls in Minneapolis, or if they do, I'm not on the guest list."

"No Natchez ball would be complete without the heiress of Blackthorn," Marcus said, leaning down to assist her to her feet. "Now let's get some dinner so you can get your beauty rest. You have to save yourself for tomorrow. Shopping and dancing all in one day. I hope you're up to it!"

"Even with a mask on, I'll know you," Aurelia vowed.

"How?"

"You can't resist teasing me." She lifted her eyebrows. "But behind a mask, I just might tease you back."

ABBOT'S RIB HOUSE was casual in atmosphere, but Aurelia had never tasted anything so heavenly as the barbecued ribs. She was almost embarrassed by the mountain of bones that had accumulated in front of her.

"If I don't stop eating like this, I won't be able to find a ball gown in my size," she said.

Marcus lifted one of her barbecue-sauce laden hands and held it up. With great deliberation he felt one of her fingers. "No, I think a little more meat on the bones is necessary.'' He winked at her. ''I learned that from the wicked witch.''

''If I'm Gretel, where's Hansel?'' she asked.

''In the oven?''

''Oh!'' She threw a napkin at him. She was about to tell him that he should have children, with his love of fairy tales and mischief, but she stopped herself. He'd made it very clear that he had no desire to shoulder more responsibility. That was something she knew far too well. But the thought of children reminded her of the crying baby in the woods.

''Marcus, what do you know about ghostly infants at Blackthorn?'' She could see by his reaction that her question had unsettled him. He put down the rib he was about to eat.

''You're not still worried about Yvonne Harris's crazy story, are you?''

''No, and don't play innocent with me,'' she said. ''I know you know every possible tale about Blackthorn. You said a baby died in the sixties or seventies? Surely there have been other reports of people hearing it?''

''In all the years I've been around Blackthorn, I've never heard a baby. It's probably two trees rubbing together or a piece of tin screeching in the wind.''

Aurelia leveled her gaze at Marcus. ''Tell me the story.''

He sighed. ''I told you about the poor infant left by the hippies who camped up there, but there is one other story. Back in the 1860s, someone left an infant in the woods near Blackthorn. Rachel Agee found the babe, almost dead from starvation and exposure. She took her in and adopted her. The child, Lilly I think was her name, was raised as an Agee.''

''And what happened to the baby's mother?''

Marcus gazed down at his plate. ''They found her dead.''

''In the woods at Blackthorn?''

''Yes.''

''How did she die?'' Aurelia felt as if her ribs had closed against her lungs. She could feel her heart pounding. It was all legend and folklore, but it was still having an unpleasant effect on her. ''Tell me, Marcus.''

''Her throat was cut.''

''And the father?''

''He never admitted the child was his.''

''The girl was unmarried?''

''Yes, she was a servant in the home of a wealthy family, one of the carpetbagger families. She was from a good family who'd lost everything during the war and Reconstruction.''

''And nothing was ever done to the child's father?''

Marcus met her gaze. ''He moved away.''

''Just like that, he simply left?'' Aurelia didn't believe it and she knew Marcus was holding out on her.

''His home was burned. He and his family nearly died in the blaze. There was a note stuck to a tree outside his burning home that told him to leave or watch his family die one by one.''

"And you believe Andre was behind that?''

Marcus nodded. "There's no proof, but I believe it. The poor girl had been raped and impregnated—some people in town knew what was happening to her but no one stepped in to stop it. The story goes that she hid her pregnancy and when it was time to deliver, she was so afraid she hid in the thick woods at Blackthorn. Her employer hunted her down and killed her shortly after she gave birth. Somehow she was able to hide the infant. Luckily, Rachel found the child the next morning when she was riding. She heard it crying in the woods.''

"How can you be so certain of all that?'' Aurelia asked.

Marcus shook his head slowly. "The history of Blackthorn has been my obsession for a long time now. I've researched documents, talked to older residents who knew tidbits here and there. I've worked on this for years now, Aurelia.''

"But you can't prove any of this, can you?''

"Not in a legal sense. But I believe it, and so do most of the people around here.''

"It's an interesting story, but it sort of defies what you said about Andre as a nonviolent highwayman.''

"I said Andre provided the justice that was missing in Mississippi during that time. The man who killed his servant would never have been brought to justice under the judicial system in place at that time. Andre did what needed to be done.''

''So you believe in vigilante justice?''

Marcus sighed. ''Not now, Aurelia. Now we have a legal system that, for the most part, works.''

She realized how close she'd come to opening Marcus's old wound, so she changed course slightly. ''And this child, Lilly, what became of her?''

''From all accounts I've been able to dig up, she grew up with Rachel and Jacques, Andre's son. When she was old enough, she went to France. Chances are, her family is there now.''

Aurelia nodded. ''Did she know she was adopted?''

''I can't say for certain, but I think Rachel would have told her.''

Aurelia finally smiled. ''You seem to know Andre and his family very well.''

Marcus returned her smile. ''I feel that I do. But then that's the curse of historians. We identify with our subjects. How about a walk along the river before I take you home?''

LYING IN BED, Aurelia closed her eyes and remembered the gentle kiss Marcus had given her before he left. She'd been sorely tempted to invite him into the cottage for a nightcap, but she hadn't. The drive back to town was dangerous without the effects of alcohol. The main reason, though, was that she might have invited him to stay the night.

She wanted to sleep with him. It was irrational and totally out of character. She was a person who thought things through, who never let her emotions put her in a position to pay consequences that were too high. Sleeping with Marcus would be a rash and selfish thing to do. She was leaving Natchez. Her destiny was in Minneapolis. To sleep with Marcus and then leave would cost her far too much. Nonetheless, she wanted to.

Snuggling deeper under the quilts, she imagined what it would be like. He was a handsome man, strong and muscular. He would be magnificent without his clothes on. Would he still think she was beautiful if he saw her naked? The idea of it sent delicious chills all over her body. She had so little experience with men. She'd had a few dates in high school, but caring for her mother hadn't given her a lot of opportunities to spend time with men. With anyone, for that matter, except for the nurses and co-workers at the various jobs she worked. She didn't even really have a good friend in Minneapolis. In the short time she'd been in Natchez, she'd had more contact with people than she had in the past.

She realized with a pang that she didn't want to go home. She wanted to stay in Natchez. She loved Blackthorn, and the idea of what it might become. The vision of it paved and turned into a mall gave her great pain. But there was nothing else to do. It had to be sold, and she had to go back to care for her mother. There was nothing else for it, and to daydream and fantasize about a different future would only bring her more pain.

She got up and went to put on the kettle for a cup of tea. She was restless. No matter how she tried to discipline her thoughts, they returned again to Marcus. Would she know him at the ball?

The idea of the dance sent another wave of thrill and anxiety through her. She was going and she would have a wonderful time. She'd go home with some memories, at least.

She was pouring the water into her cup when she heard something outside the cottage window. The gown she wore was floor-length and flannel, yet she felt suddenly exposed. There were no curtains on the windows. Anyone could look in and see her.

See that she was alone and unarmed!

She doused the light and scurried back into the bedroom. The sound of the footsteps was distinct. Someone was walking around the cottage.

Aurelia thought of the phone and the downed lines. Marcus had said he would report the problem. She tried the phone, but it was still dead. Damn! She couldn't even call for help. She was completely on her own.

Terrified, she slipped beside the bed and the wall and hid. It was futile. Whoever was out there knew she was inside. It wouldn't take much of a search to reveal her hiding place. She pulled several quilts on top of her.

As she listened, the footsteps went around the cabin to the front. She held her breath, waiting to hear the door kicked open. Instead, there was the sound of breaking glass—and then nothing.

Chapter Seven

Aurelia watched as the man from the glass shop put in a new pane.

"That should take care of it," he said. "You might consider changing out the windows for double-paned-insulated. The summers here are brutal. You'll lose a lot of expensive cold air through these panes."

"Thank you," Aurelia said. If she were planning to stay in the cottage, she would consider new windows. But that wasn't the case.

"What happened, ma'am?"

The glass man was curious, like the rest of Natchez, and Aurelia had already made up her mind not to feed the gossip mill. Someone was deliberately trying to terrorize her, and she wasn't going to let on that it was working.

"I was sweeping and I struck the glass with the end of the broom." She gave a helpless shrug.

"Too bad." He looked at the new window as if he wondered how anyone could be that clumsy.

Aurelia wrote out a check and handed it to him. "Thank you."

When he was gone, she put on her coat and gloves and began the process of checking around the cottage. There were no footprints that she could find, but that didn't mean anything. The person who had thrown the rock through her window was a live human being, no ghost. Ghosts didn't write threatening notes.

After she'd checked all around the cottage without results, she went back inside and picked up the rock that had been wrapped with a note.

She uncrumpled the paper, realizing that in her panic last night, she'd obliterated any fingerprints that might have been on the paper. Had she been thinking, she wouldn't have touched the rock at all. Now it was too late for forensics, and she wasn't certain she should report the incident. Natchez was a hotbed of talk. Was someone trying to run her off or simply trying to lower the selling price of Blackthorn? Whichever, she had no intention of playing into his or her hands by rushing to the sheriff and acting afraid.

The note was plain white typing paper and black magic marker, block printing. "Leave Blackthorn now or die."

Anger washed over her, and she knew her normally fair skin was red. One thing her tormenter hadn't counted on was that such tactics had the opposite effect on her. Someone was trying to force her to leave

Blackthorn immediately, so she would stay until she completed her work.

She picked up the phone, surprised to see that the dial tone was back. Marcus apparently had some pull with the phone company to get a truck on the job so rapidly. She called Yvonne Harris and left word that she would be away from Blackthorn for the morning. The appraiser would have to wait until afternoon.

Eager to shop, she got her keys and drove into town. She had a ball gown to buy. She was going to Killburn Estate and would act as if nothing untoward had occurred at Blackthorn.

Three hours later, with the most incredibly beautiful dress she'd ever owned stowed in the trunk of her car, Aurelia found herself starving. She'd thrown caution to the wind and bought new shoes, too. Dazzling shoes.

She drove to the café where Marcus had taken her and pulled into the crowded parking lot. Ella Jensen had a steady crowd all day long, apparently. The smell of pork chops was almost more than she could bear as she hurried inside and took a seat at the counter.

"Aurelia," Ella greeted her with a smile.

"What a crowd!" Aurelia noticed that every table was full.

"Pork chops, field peas, corn bread, fried okra and sweet-potato fluff. It's always a favorite."

"I want all of it," Aurelia said, slightly embarrassed at her greed. "A lot of all of it."

Ella laughed out loud. "You can stand a little meat on your bones. I'll throw in some pecan pie for desert."

Aurelia thought she might swoon. She sipped the sweetened iced tea a waitress put in front of her.

In only a few moments, she was tucking into the steaming plate of food. Never in her life had she eaten anything so delicious. To her amazement, she found her plate clean and Ella standing behind the counter, smiling at her.

"What about that pie?"

Aurelia groaned. "Bring it on," she said. "Or maybe you should stop me before I hurt myself."

Ella put a piece of pie on the counter. "How are things at Blackthorn?"

"Fine," Aurelia said. She hated lying to Ella, but she couldn't risk telling anyone about the broken window and the threat.

"Marcus said your phone lines were down last night. He called and reported it."

"They already fixed them." Last night, she might have called the sheriff, if she'd been able.

"That old estate means a lot of things to a lot of people," Ella said. She pulled a stool out from under the counter and took a seat. "I'm going to take a break and talk to you for a minute if you don't mind."

Aurelia was glad for the company. She liked Ella. "Marcus said you knew stories about Andre."

"I'm sure he's told you most of what I know."

Ella's brown eyes were troubled. "I heard about the fracas with Lottie Levert."

"Did you hear that I pushed her down?" Aurelia slowly lowered her fork to the saucer.

"Yes. I heard you threatened her and then attacked her." Ella shook her head. "Of course, I didn't believe it. No one in his right mind would believe such a foolish story."

"But it is being repeated, even by those who don't believe it. That's the nature of gossip." Aurelia was finding her introduction to small-town celebrity a bitter experience. For the most part, her life had been sheltered from public scrutiny.

"I'm sorry. But it'll blow over. What I suggest is that you keep a wide berth from Lottie. I wouldn't put it past her to jump in front of your car and then accuse you of trying to run her down."

Aurelia laughed, though she was troubled by what Ella was saying.

"Let's talk about something more fun. Marcus tells me you're going to the Killburn ball."

"I bought my gown today." Despite her worries, Aurelia couldn't help feeling the excitement.

"Wonderful. Let me guess, the dress is forest green with emerald faux feather trim." She laughed at the expression on Aurelia's face.

"How did you know?"

"Sometimes I see things. Just a glimpse of the past or future. I had a vivid picture of you in that dress in a dream last night." She put a hand on Aurelia's.

"Honey, don't look at me like I'm some kind of demon. It's just a little gift."

"Do you see anything else?" Aurelia asked, the words almost sticking in her throat.

"I see a big commotion up at Blackthorn. You're safe, and so is Marcus. But there are red and blue lights flashing, folks gathered up, all worried."

"Was there an accident?" Aurelia found she was holding her breath. Red and blue lights generally meant trouble.

"I can't say. I just had a flash of it last night, like I saw you in that dress. That was it, just a brief glimpse."

Aurelia pulled money from her pocket and slowly picked up the ticket. "I don't know if I should thank you or not," she said, forcing a laugh.

"I debated whether I should tell you. Marcus told me I should. He said you had a right to know."

"Do the things you see always come true?"

"I can't answer that, honey. Some things I see involve people I don't know or places I've never been. I have no way of checking to see what happened."

"The times you see people around here. Are the visions true?"

Ella took a slow breath. "For the most part."

"What happened at Blackthorn?"

"I can't say for certain," Ella said cautiously. "But I clearly saw you and Marcus, and neither of you were hurt."

Aurelia felt a smidgen of relief, but she was still

troubled by Ella's vision. "When is this supposed to happen, if it happens?"

Ella shook her head. "I don't know."

Aurelia gathered her purse. "Thanks for telling me, Ella. I'll be careful."

"That's the only reason I told you. Marcus said I ought to."

"He was right. I need to know these things." But as Aurelia walked out the door of the diner, she wasn't certain what had motivated Marcus or his friend, Ella.

DESPITE EVERYTHING, Aurelia felt her heart lift as her rental car climbed the steep drive to Blackthorn. Every time she drove back, she saw something new and beautiful. The path was overgrown, but if the underbrush was cut back, the drive would be lined with magnificent oaks and magnolias. Blackthorn had been neglected, but a loving hand and a bit of money could easily bring the property back. Perhaps the land could be rented. Would that generate enough income to pay her mother's bills? Aurelia thought not, but it was something she'd check into.

She was surprised to see a white Land Rover in the drive in front of the cottage until she remembered that the appraiser was supposed to arrive. He was early, and she was a little late.

He got out of his vehicle as soon as she pulled up. "Charlie Smoke," he said, extending his hand. "This is quite a piece of property, at least according to the map.'' He showed her the piece of paper that clearly marked the boundaries of Blackthorn.

"I'd like to walk with you," she said. "I haven't really seen the property either."

"Glad for the company. Yvonne said the place is haunted." He gave a doubtful look. "Yvonne may have had one or two martinis too many before she came."

Aurelia instantly liked Charlie Smoke. He was a wiry man with gold-rimmed glasses. They started at the cottage, walked through the woods, and circled back to where the old pillars marked the location of the original mansion.

"These pillars are beautiful," Charlie said. "I've heard about this place since I moved to Natchez."

"So you aren't a native?"

"No, I've only been here twenty years. It'll probably take my children's children to be accepted." He was teasing, but Aurelia knew it was partially true.

"And what do you make of all the stories about Blackthorn?"

"Local legends that give the area a little spice. Everywhere I've lived there's always been a haunted house. Blackthorn isn't haunted, but it makes a good story."

"I quite agree," Aurelia said, pushing aside, for the moment, the things she'd seen and heard on the property.

They continued walking and passed the thicket of devil's walking sticks. "Nasty-looking plants," Charlie said. "Now over this way should be the Indian burial mound."

Aurelia followed him down a narrow trail through dense undergrowth until they came to what looked like a man-made hillock of grass-covered dirt. It was strangely out of place. As she drew closer, she saw holes had been dug in it. Many of them were older, but several looked very fresh.

"Hunting for the treasure," Charlie said. "They'll never give up. They don't realize they're vandalizing a sacred burial ground."

"Are you Native American?"

He gave her a sidelong glance. "Just a whisper of Cherokee. My people come from north of here. The tribes around here were Choctaw, Chickasaw, Mound Builders. This mound here is allegedly the burial site of one of the great leaders, Wenabitta. It's a very sacred place."

Aurelia sat down on a fallen tree beside the mound. "Is the site valuable?"

"To anthropologists, historians, those who love the history of the land. And to the remaining Mound Builders. But financially, no. I'm sure once you sell Blackthorn, the bulldozers will flatten this mound in no time."

Aurelia walked around the base of it. It was huge, about half as big as a football field. Charlie walked beside her, noting the places where some treasure hunter had dug. Some of the holes were deep. Others had filled in over time.

"They're always looking for a treasure," Charlie said sadly. "By the way, John Ittawasa was in the office this morning. He's the head of the remaining Mound Builders. He was upset to hear I was coming out to appraise Blackthorn. I wouldn't be surprised if he doesn't try to mount some opposition to the sale of the estate."

"He has no right to do that," Aurelia said. Why were everyone and his brother attempting to put a finger in her business?

"He thinks he does."

"How did he even hear about the proposed sale? I haven't advertised at all. Yet."

"Now that's a good question. But anyone could have called him."

"He doesn't live in Natchez?" Aurelia was shocked.

"Oh, no, he lives in Philadelphia, Mississippi, on the reservation there. He said he got a call from someone."

"Natchez seems to be a place where people delight in minding others' business," Aurelia said.

Charlie turned to her. "The rest of the property was once in cotton or woods. Most of it's overgrown and hard to walk through. I've seen enough to work up an estimate for you, but I can say off the top of my head that the half million Leon is offering you is too low.

"How did you know—"

"Everyone in Natchez knows what Kimball offered. He's tight as a tick. Tell him no and wait for a better offer.'' Charlie leaned closer to her, his eyes wide. ''But don't tell him I told you that. He's a vindictive man.''

MARCUS STOOD AT a strategic point where he could watch the door for Aurelia's arrival. No matter if she wore a mask. He'd know her anywhere, under any circumstances.

He wasn't the only one watching, though, when she swept through the front door. Half of Natchez society took note. An approving murmur swept through the crowd.

Before Marcus could step to Aurelia's side, Amy Wintzel had her arm. ''You are the spitting image of Rachel Agee,'' Amy said in a whisper that was designed to carry. ''No one ever thought her beauty could be equaled, but they were wrong.''

Marcus took a deep breath. Amy was a troublemaker of the highest order. She obviously wanted everyone in the room to know who Aurelia was.

He stepped forward and took Aurelia's arm. The small orchestra was playing a waltz. ''May I?'' he asked, sweeping her away before she could answer.

He was surprised to find Aurelia so stiff in his arms. ''It's me, Marcus,'' he said, wondering if she'd failed to recognize him.

''I know who it is,'' she said crisply. ''What I want to know is if you called John Ittawasa to try and block the sale of Blackthorn?''

Aurelia's green eyes were furious through her mask. Marcus danced her to the edge of the ballroom floor and then whisked her out a side door onto a brick patio. "I told John the property was going to be sold. I didn't sic him on you."

"What did you think would happen? That he would just stand aside and let that burial mound be destroyed?"

"I hoped he might be able to shake some money out of the state legislature to preserve the mound."

Aurelia was so angry her chest was moving rapidly in and out. He had to convince her that he was trying to help.

"I never intended—"

She broke in before he could finish. "John Ittawasa may be the one person who can block the sale of Blackthorn. I'm sure that didn't slip by you." She bit her bottom lip. "I have to sell the estate. I have to. My mother's care depends on it." She turned around abruptly.

Marcus knew she was about to cry, and he knew better than to touch her. She was too upset. He also knew that he had to make her believe he hadn't been trying to derail her plans to sell Blackthorn when he made the call to the chief.

"Aurelia, I do want to preserve Blackthorn. But that isn't my top priority. If the estate has to be sold, then it has to. I sincerely hoped that John could get the money. I didn't believe anyone else with an interest in preserving the estate had a chance. So I called him.''

''And what if he delays the sale for an extended period?''

''I don't know. We'll figure something out.''

Aurelia started by Marcus. She stopped and looked up at him. ''I'm selling to Leon Kimball tomorrow. It's the only option I have. Then he can worry about the chief and the burial mound.''

She brushed past him and disappeared into the throng of masked dancers. A moment later she was in a man's arms dancing another waltz. Marcus stared at the man. He couldn't be certain, but he bore a strong resemblance in size and shape to Leon Kimball.

Chapter Eight

Aurelia was in the middle of her third dance before the anger abated. She had no idea who her previous partners had been—and didn't care. Though she'd suspected one was Leon Kimball, she hadn't broached the subject of selling Blackthorn to him. She'd do so in the morning in a more appropriate place.

The dance ended and her tall partner bowed slightly as he left her at the edge of the dance floor. She saw Marcus walking toward her and she hurried away. Her anger was too great. His motivation might have been to preserve Blackthorn, as he claimed, but his strategy was one that could cripple her from selling the estate. If Chief John Ittawasa was able to get the burial ground declared a sacred place, then Blackthorn could never be developed. She understood that. She'd read about such cases in the newspaper. Perhaps Marcus hadn't intended for that to be the result, but his meddling could cause great damage.

"Miss Agee, may I have this dance?"

She turned to find herself staring at a man of average height. "How did you know my name?" she asked.

"Everyone in this room is talking about your beauty," he said smoothly as he took her hand and tucked it around his elbow.

She allowed him to escort her to the dance floor. In a moment she was in his arms and dancing. Though she studied him, she couldn't remember ever meeting him before. The mask concealed everything but his eyes, which were watching her with a strange glint.

"I believe we have something in common," he said.

"What would that be?"

"My mother," he said with a quick shake of his head. "Lottie Levert. I'm Randall."

"Oh," Aurelia stopped herself from further comment.

"My mother has always been determined to have Blackthorn. She told me about meeting you, and what happened."

Aurelia didn't respond, but she was aware that Randall Levert had increased the pressure on her back as he drew her closer to him. She tried to think of something to say, but there was nothing. Lottie Levert had no real claim to the property. If she did, she would have acted on it long ago.

"What are your plans for the estate?" Randall Levert asked.

Once again Aurelia felt a surge of anxiety. "Disposition of the estate is strictly my business," she said, making it clear.

"What are your plans?" he asked again.

"Blackthorn will be sold," she said in a tone that brooked no argument.

"Have you any offers?"

This man was incredible. He had more gall than anyone she'd ever met.

"Yes."

"May I ask who has offered?"

"No, you may not," she said, stopping in the middle of the dance floor. "I'm tired. Thank you for the dance." She stiffly walked away feeling as if every eye in the room was on her. So much for her grand dream of a ball. She started toward the balcony where she hoped for a moment of quiet.

She was surprised to feel a hand on her upper arm, pulling her around. She turned to face Randall Levert, and there was anger in his eyes.

"Don't walk away from me."

"Let me go," she said as calmly as she could.

"What if my mother's claim is right? What if she *is* the rightful heir of Blackthorn?"

"If her claim were valid she would have acted on it long before I came here," Aurelia said. She was now truly the focus of everyone's attention. "Let go of my arm."

"This isn't over," Randall said loudly. He leaned forward and lowered his voice. "There are legal issues here. You won't be selling Blackthorn any time soon. I'm going to get an injunction to stop you. When and if you do sell Blackthorn, my mother will get her rightful share.''

"Or what?" Aurelia asked.

"Andre Agee rides that land. I'd be careful if I tried to swindle his blood.''

MARCUS HEARD ONLY the tail end of the conversation, but it was enough to make him step forward. "Randall, I didn't think you were fool enough to believe your mother's claims.''

"I heard you were looking for me," Randall said nastily. "You've done everything in your power to align yourself with this interloper. You think you can influence her to save your precious Blackthorn. Well, she's selling it.''

Marcus didn't bother to respond. He turned to make sure Aurelia was okay, but she was already walking out of the room. Even from that distance he could see the flush on her bare arms and shoulders. She was embarrassed and angry, and he didn't blame her. Randall had made a scene.

He turned back to the car salesman. "Blackthorn isn't mine or yours. Aurelia can do what she likes with it, and it's time everyone in this town acknowledges that. For years the estate has sat empty. No one cared. Now, all of a sudden, it's all everyone can talk about. Including me. Well it's time to back off and let Aurelia do as she wishes. It's hers.''

He spoke loud enough so everyone in the room could hear. When he was finished, he started after Aurelia. He owed her an apology. Calling John Ittawasa had been out of line.

By the time he got to the parking lot, Aurelia was already driving away. He watched as her car lights disappeared down the long drive. This hadn't been the way he'd hoped the night would end. The wisest course of action, though, was to leave her alone and let her calm down. She'd been publicly embarrassed, though he had to admire the starch in her spine.

When he returned to the party, he searched the crowd for Leon and Randall. Both were gone. He'd hoped to have a word, privately, with each of them making it clear that they were to leave Aurelia alone.

"Marcus," Amy Wintzel said in a long drawl as she took his arm. "Dance with me."

"What's the purpose of the masks if you call everyone by name?" he asked her as he allowed her to lead him to the dance floor.

"It's tradition," she said archly. "You know how important tradition is in Natchez. And speaking of which, what is the true story on our lovely little heiress?"

Marcus sighed. "She's smart and beautiful and the owner of Blackthorn. That's all I can tell you."

"Did she really threaten Lottie Levert?"

Marcus wanted to shake Amy. It was exactly this kind of stupid gossip that made extraordinary trouble in people's lives. Case in point was Wade Gammit.

Everyone in town heard rumors that he was violent and had a grudge against a man who was killed. The rumors were so prevalent that an eyewitness who saw the murder identified Wade. Yet Wade was innocent.

"Aurelia didn't threaten anyone. You know Lottie is crazy. Apparently it runs in the family. Please don't repeat malicious gossip, Amy. It makes you look ugly."

He could see she was affronted by his remark, but she was far too accomplished a gossipmonger to be put off. "But she pushed Lottie to the ground. She pushed an old woman down. She could have broken her hip or something."

"She didn't push Lottie down and you know it. Amy, what you're doing is wrong. Why are you so damn jealous of Aurelia that you need to damage her reputation?"

No matter how smooth Amy was, she couldn't hide the anger that leaped into her eyes. "How dare you? I'm not jealous of that little twit."

"Ah, but you are," he said, putting slight pressure on the hand that she'd tucked in the crook of his elbow. "You're so jealous you'd repeat things you know aren't true. Stop it now, Amy. There is such a thing as slander, which is prosecutable."

"You know the law, Marcus, you just don't have the guts to practice it." Amy pulled her hand free and marched away.

To his aggravation, Marcus realized that he'd once

again fumbled his attempt to protect Aurelia. Hard as it was to accept, it would be best if he left her alone.

BY THE TIME she reached the turnoff to her drive, Aurelia was calm. She only wanted to get out of the fancy dress, find her nightgown and forget the entire night. What a waste of time, money and effort. She'd gotten herself all dressed up just so she could be the focus of a threat by a maniac. Were all the people of Natchez nuts? Maybe she should buy bottled water in the morning, just in case.

She drove slowly up the steep incline, trying to force her body to relax. Soon she would finish up with selling Blackthorn. Then she could go home.

The problem was that Minneapolis wasn't really home anymore. It was simply where her mother was being kept. The small cottage at Blackthorn felt more like home.

That distressing thought was foremost in her mind as she parked and hurried inside. The night had grown bitterly cold. As she was locking the door behind her, she noticed that there were no stars in the sky. A storm was brewing. It didn't really matter. She would be snug inside the cottage even if the windows weren't insulated.

Andre Agee wouldn't dare disturb her sleep tonight. And if the mysterious intruder who'd broken her window decided to return, Aurelia had decided she'd instantly call the police. In fact, in the morning she was going straight to the sheriff's office to report the broken window and Randall Levert's threats. She'd been foolish not to report everything. And she was also going by Yvonne Harris's. Charlie Smoke said he'd have the appraisal ready. It was time to put Blackthorn on the auction block. It was time to put an end to her sojourn in Natchez.

AURELIA AWOKE BEFORE dawn when the entire cottage trembled in the wake of thunder. She got out of bed and added more wood to the fireplace. When she went to the window, she could see the wind whipping through the trees and lightning flashing over the river. It was one of the most stupendous thunderstorms she'd ever witnessed. She could only thank her lucky stars that she was inside, warm and dry.

Instead of going back to bed, she moved one of the rocking chairs to the window so she could watch the fiery display in the sky. Bolts of lightning with up to five prongs split the sky. Since the fireworks seemed to be some distance away, Aurelia simply enjoyed it. In Minneapolis, she lived in the middle of the city. Of course they had storms, but none with the pristine beauty of this one. In the city the lights were always on; the stark beauty of a black night could never be seen.

The storm passed, but Aurelia was unable to sleep. She made coffee, bathed and dressed. When dawn cracked the sky, she went outside and walked through the freshly washed woods. Blackthorn was even more beautiful with the ice crystals sparkling in the bare trees.

When she decided it was a reasonable time to go into town, she returned to the cottage. She decided to call Yvonne first, but when she picked up the phone, the line was dead once again. Sighing, she knew she'd have to call the repair service herself. She was no longer willing to rely on Marcus for anything. It was, indeed, time she left Natchez.

She drove slowly down the drive, aware of the ice. She hadn't bothered to listen to news or weather reports since her arrival in the river city. Now she wondered how cold it had gotten during the storm.

Her first stop was Yvonne's. The Realtor was slightly harried, but she agreed to set up an auction on the property the following Saturday It would be only two days to wait, and Aurelia conceded to that necessity. Yvonne promised to call all the large developers in the Southeast, as well as anyone else who might be interested.

Feeling as if she'd agreed to sell a family member, Aurelia decided to walk through the town to the courthouse. In the bright sunlight, the freshly washed streets were beautiful. The old brick buildings of downtown looked like they'd come out of a painting. As she walked, she noticed the wrought-iron work that gave the city a festive feel. Was this Ella's heritage? she wondered.

The courthouse was old and lovely. Walking inside, she found the door marked for the sheriff's office. When she asked to see the sheriff, she was immediately sent to a large office where a dark-haired man in his midthirties sat at a desk heaped with paperwork.

"Good morning," he said as he looked up. "Can I help you?"

He looked far too young to be a sheriff.

"My father was sheriff," he said as if he read her mind. "I inherited the position, sort of."

"Sheriffs are elected." Aurelia was surprised that she knew that fact. She normally wasn't at all interested in politics.

"I know. My dad got sick and I finished out his term. Folks asked me to stay on." He grinned.

It was a charming way of saying he'd won an election, and Aurelia grinned back. Some of the people in Natchez were mighty nice, and this lawman seemed to be one of them.

"Dru Colson," he said, holding out his hand.

"Aurelia Agee." She shook firmly.

"Ah, the heiress." He pointed to a chair. "The whole town is buzzing about you."

"So I've heard."

"Lottie Levert came by to file a complaint."

The sheriff was still friendly, but he was also assessing her.

"I didn't touch her."

"Lottie can be a little...eccentric."

Aurelia didn't say that Lottie was just plain crazy, though she thought it.

"Sheriff, someone has been on my property." She pulled the rock and note out of her coat pocket. "They broke my window night before last and left this."

He studied the note carefully. "Too bad you picked it up."

"I know."

"I'll send a deputy up to take a look at things."

"I'd appreciate it, sheriff. My telephone's been going out and it makes me a little more anxious than I normally am."

Dru Colson stood up. "I'll send a deputy this morning. I hope the remainder of your stay in Natchez is without incident."

"Thank you." Aurelia was headed for the door when it burst open. Randall Levert rushed into the room, pulling up short when he saw her.

"What have you done to my mother!" He started toward her, but the sheriff smoothly stepped into his path.

"What's the problem, Randall?"

"My mother is gone. And that woman right there knows something about it."

Aurelia was too stunned to protest.

"What are you talking about?" Dru's tone wasn't very gentle. "What's Lottie up to now?"

"My mother isn't up to anything. She's missing. I went by her house this morning and she wasn't there."

"Was her car gone?" Dru asked calmly.

"Of course her car was gone! That's what I'm try-ing to tell you. My mother is gone!"

"Have you checked the grocery stores?" Dru kept his focus directly on Randall, but Aurelia thought she caught a hint of a smile at the corners of his mouth.

"My mother doesn't grocery shop at eight in the morning!"

"Hair salon, doctor's office, post office, tax asses-sor," Dru began to tick off possible places Lottie could be.

"My mother never leaves the house early in the morning," Randall said doggedly. "She sleeps in, then has her coffee, and finally runs her errands in the afternoon. I know my mother's habits. Something is wrong."

For the first time since Randall burst into the room, Aurelia saw there was worry in Dru's face. "Are you sure?"

"I've known my mother for thirty-eight years. She'd rather take a beating than get up early and go out."

"What about the hospital? Maybe she felt ill?" Dru asked.

"I called the emergency room. No sign of her."

"Normal procedure is to wait twenty-four hours on a missing person," Dru said, "but I'll have my dep-uties look out for her. What kind of car does she drive?"

"It's a red Cadillac Eldorado." Randall turned to-ward Aurelia. "Did you see Mother?"

"No," Aurelia said. She almost stepped back from the ferocity of Randall's question.

Dru took a step forward so Randall had to step back. "I'll alert the deputies. If we find the car, where will you be?"

Randall gave the sheriff his cell phone number. "I'll be looking for my mother. And the first place I'm going to check is Blackthorn. Unless you have some objection." Randall spoke to Aurelia rather than the sheriff.

"Go ahead and look all you want. I haven't seen your mother and have no desire to see her."

Randall slammed the office door as he was leaving. Aurelia found she was exhausted by the exchange. She sank back down in the chair.

"Are you okay?" Dru asked.

"I'll be very glad to execute the sale of Blackthorn and go back to Minnesota," she said.

"Let me get you a cup of coffee," Dru said. "It won't take but a minute."

Aurelia didn't argue. She closed her eyes as the sheriff left his office and went in search of fresh, hot coffee.

In less than ten minutes, he was back, a steaming cup of coffee in both hands. He held both out to her. "Black or cream and sugar, take your pick."

"Black," she said.

"Good, because I like mine sweet and light." He handed her the cup of black coffee. "Let me tell you a little about your family estate."

"Go right ahead," she said, sipping the coffee. It seemed everyone in town had something to say about Blackthorn. She might as well see what the sheriff's story was.

"Blackthorn is something of a town possession," Dru said, taking a seat on the edge of his desk. In the next fifteen minutes he recounted the history of the estate much as Marcus had told her. "I'm sorry this has been so hard for you. Is there anything I can do to help?" Dru concluded.

"I've called Yvonne Harris. I'm going to auction the estate this Saturday. Just make sure nothing happens to gum up the works between now and Saturday." She gave a halfhearted smile. "Then I'm heading north."

"Once again, I'm sorry this has been difficult. But it'll all be over in a few days."

The telephone on his desk began to ring. He picked it up and spoke, then listened. His gaze shifted to Aurelia, and there was a questioning light in his eyes. "Tell Randall I'll be up there with some deputies and volunteers. If Lottie's in the woods, we'll find her."

When he put the phone down he turned to Aurelia. "Randall called in. His mother's car is parked on the side road on the northern border of Blackthorn property. There's no sign of Lottie."

Chapter Nine

Marcus listened to Dru Colson as he explained the quadrants of the search. The sheriff was tense. One of the local businessmen had reported seeing Lottie's car at midnight parked along County Road 32 that made up the northern border of the estate. "There's a possibility that Mrs. Levert has spent the entire night in the woods, and it was a bitter, cold night," Dru said. "We need to get this search going right away."

"She did something to my mother." Randall pointed at Aurelia, who had also volunteered to search. It hadn't escaped Marcus that Aurelia had been teamed with a deputy.

Aurelia ignored Randall, but Marcus could see that it cost her. He walked over to her, wary of the reception he might receive. In her place, he'd feel as if everyone in town was out to get him.

"Are you okay?" he asked.

Her full lips turned up at one corner. "I'm being accused of making a middle-aged woman disappear."

"No one in his right mind would believe that."

She looked around at the group of men and women who had come to search. "Every single person here wants to believe it. I'm an outsider, an interloper. There's absolutely no telling what awful practices we Minnesotans have. We probably eat our young."

Marcus laughed softly, and Aurelia's face eased. "I'll warn the other searchers," he said.

"Good. Maybe then they'll stay away from me and leave me alone."

"Aurelia, did you see or hear anything last night?"

"Sheriff Colson's already asked all the pertinent questions. There was such a storm last night an army of banshees could have been wailing in the front yard and I wouldn't have heard them."

"It was a bad storm. February brings the worst in weather. If it keeps raining, the river will flood. Of course, Blackthorn is perfectly safe. The bluffs protect you. The other side of the river tends to have the flooding problems."

He saw that his casual conversation was easing her anxiety, and he determined he'd ask Dru to let him stay with Aurelia. The sheriff would comply.

"Who's that?" Aurelia asked, indicating a tall man with long dark hair streaked with gray.

"That's John Ittawasa."

Aurelia sighed. "Great. Everyone's here to see the wicked heiress found guilty of some crime or other."

"John's an excellent tracker. If anyone can find

Lottie, he can. He's studied the skills of the woodsmen. I think the sheriff asked him to help.''

"Oh." Aurelia shifted her weight. "I'm sorry, Marcus. I'm beginning to develop a persecution complex, I think."

"It's understandable. Look, we're getting ready to search. Come on."

They fell into place and as the line spread out and started moving forward, Marcus kept an eye on both Aurelia and John Ittawasa, as much as he could. Randall was too far away to watch, and that troubled Marcus. He didn't trust the man. In fact, he wouldn't be surprised to discover that this entire disappearance was some act Randall and Lottie had concocted together to make things tough for Aurelia. It was exactly the sort of high drama Lottie loved.

Through the thick woods, Dru's radio crackled. There was indistinct conversation and then silence. In a moment, Dru appeared at Marcus's elbow.

"I need to talk to you a minute."

The two men fell back and Aurelia continued forward, searching the ground for any sign of Lottie.

"What is it?" Marcus asked, immediately concerned by the expression on Dru's face.

"That was Penelope House, the women's abuse center. Lottie was scheduled to work the hotline for them yesterday evening and she didn't show up. They said she's never missed a single time."

"That's not good," Marcus said, immediately aware of what the sheriff was getting at. Lottie had been out of pocket for almost eighteen hours. That was a long time if she'd been injured in the Blackthorn woods.

"Has Aurelia said anything to you?"

That question revealed the depth of the sheriff's concern, and it made Marcus even more worried. He and Dru had been friends throughout high school and their professional lives. "She hasn't said anything regarding Lottie. I believe her, Dru. If Lottie's on the Blackthorn property, Aurelia doesn't know anything about it."

"You care about Miss Agee, don't you?" Dru asked.

This wasn't the time to be evasive about his feelings. "Yes," Marcus said, a little surprised at the depth of his emotion.

"This doesn't look good."

"Aurelia wouldn't harm a fly."

"Then let's hope we find Lottie cold, wet and miserable with a sprained ankle or something of that nature."

"Whatever Lottie's condition, Aurelia had nothing to do with it."

Dru kept his gaze steady on Marcus. "I have to take this seriously. Lottie filed a complaint against Aurelia. She said Aurelia had threatened her and tried to injure her. Even if I believe Lottie exaggerated, that complaint is still on the books. In a trial, you know how that would look."

And Marcus did. He knew only too well. He had

the horrible sensation that he was slipping back into the past—a past he'd done everything he could to leave behind.

AURELIA ZIPPED HER jacket up to her throat. It was bitterly cold. It would serve Lottie right if she was frozen to a solid block of ice. Aurelia immediately felt bad for her lack of charity. Even though Lottie was an awful person, she didn't deserve to freeze.

The woods at Blackthorn had taken on a different feel. This, too, was a part of the woods she'd never seen. They'd come from the northern boundary and were walking south. By her calculation, the river was at least a mile away. Instead of the wild beauty she'd seen before, the huge trees somehow seemed sinister. The crackle of dozens of feet shuffling through the underbrush reminded Aurelia of the rustling of restless spirits. She'd stayed at Blackthorn too long. She was beginning to believe the legends.

She glanced behind her to find the sheriff and Marcus still in a conversation that could only be described as intense. She wondered what had happened but knew better than to ask. No one would tell her. She was a suspect in Lottie's disappearance—even though the foolish woman had been trespassing on Blackthorn property.

She focused on the ground, looking for any sign that a human had trodden that way. In all likelihood, if Lottie had left a trail, the rain had washed it away. The search would be successful only if they stumbled on Lottie. That was a scenario Aurelia didn't think likely.

In her opinion, Lottie was sitting somewhere warm and safe, laughing about all the drama she'd created. She would be able to tell the story of the search for months to come.

"Hey! Over here!"

The cry rang out from the east where the densest part of the woods were located. Aurelia froze. She didn't know whether to go forward and see what had been found or to wait.

"Sheriff! You'd better get over here!"

That call galvanized her to action. She hurried toward the caller to see for herself what had been found.

"Mother!"

Randall Levert's anguished cry stopped her in her tracks.

"Mother!" he yelled again. "No!"

Searchers ran past Aurelia. Dread was a knot in her stomach. She'd never truly considered that Lottie was injured. But it sounded as if something horrible had happened.

Instead of going with the others, Marcus came to her side. He put his hand around her arm as if she might need support. Together they slowly walked forward to see what had been found.

At first Aurelia saw only the backs of the searchers. They were standing in a circle around something on the ground. She tried to hang back, but Marcus gently urged her forward.

"Don't act afraid," he cautioned her. "Just keep going."

When they were close, it was almost as if the men in front of her parted. She was given a clear view of Lottie Levert lying on the ground. She knew by the position of the body that Lottie was dead. Randall was kneeling beside her. His tearstained face turned to Aurelia.

"You did this. You killed my mother!"

Aurelia tried to speak but her mouth was so dry she couldn't make a sound come out. Every one of the searchers turned to look at her. She saw the accusation on their faces. She lifted a hand to protect herself, and then she felt the world spinning, the stark limbs of the huge trees a terrifying whirl as she felt her knees buckle.

MARCUS CAUGHT AURELIA before she hit the ground. Without a word to the sheriff, he swung her into his arms and began walking back to the road where he'd parked his car when the searchers had begun to work their way through the woods.

He wasn't certain what had happened to Lottie, but he had no doubt she was dead. In Blackthorn woods. If ever there had been a night for Andre Agee to ride his hell horse, last night had been it. But who would have thought Lottie Levert would have picked the coldest storm in five years to go to Blackthorn?

It was the worst possible turn of events for Aurelia. But there was no point jumping to conclusions until an autopsy was performed. If Lottie died of exposure, no blame could possibly be directed at Aurelia. Everyone in town knew Lottie was a little crazy.

The thing that had to be discovered was, what Lottie was doing at Blackthorn? What could possibly draw a middle-aged woman into the woods on a freezing, stormy night?

When he got to his car, Marcus managed to get Aurelia into the passenger seat. He wasted no time driving back to the main road and the turnoff up the steep drive that marked the entrance to Blackthorn. Aurelia was still out, but there was color in her cheeks.

Marcus was surprised to find the cottage door unlocked, and he carried Aurelia to the bed and gently put her down. He took off her hiking boots, jacket and gloves and pulled the sheet and quilts over her. She was moaning softly, her expression one of dismay. He pulled a chair beside the bed and waited. It was only a few moments when her eyes opened. Fear gave way almost immediately to confusion.

"Lottie was found in the woods, wasn't she?" she asked, sounding as if she wished it were a dream.

"She was."

"Is she really dead?"

Marcus nodded. "It's just as well you fainted, but the sheriff will be here soon enough to question you."

"How did she die?" Aurelia sat up in the bed.

"After you fainted, I didn't get a good look at the

body, but my guess is it'll take an autopsy to determine that.''

"Lying out all alone in that weather—what a horrible way to die." She pulled the sheets around her. "This is awful."

Marcus realized then that even with Randall's accusations, Aurelia had no concept of the potential danger she was in. She was innocent of any foul play in Lottie's death, but sometimes that didn't matter.

"Aurelia, they'll do an autopsy. If someone hurt Lottie, the first suspect is going to be you."

"What?" Her normally pale face blanched. "I didn't hurt her. I wouldn't go into those woods in the middle of a stormy night for anything. I'd get lost and never get out."

He put a gentle hand on her thigh. "I know that. But I'm telling you, if the sheriff comes to talk to you, don't answer any questions."

"That's ridiculous. I don't have anything to hide."

He increased his pressure on her thigh, getting her attention. "Don't say anything. Dru Colson is a good man, but anything you say will be repeated to a jury if this goes to trial. Then the meaning will be twisted and distorted by the prosecution. Trust me, I've seen it happen." He could see he was scaring her half to death, and he hoped it was sufficient to keep her mouth shut.

"I didn't do anything," she whispered. "I have to get home to my mother."

"Chances are this will turn out to be a case of death

by exposure. I'm just warning you against the worst-case scenario. Now tell me you won't talk to Dru or anyone else without a lawyer with you.''

"You're really making me afraid,'' she said, a tear trembling in her left eye.

"I'm sorry, but I'm trying to protect you.''

"Where was Andre Agee last night?'' Aurelia asked with a flash of anger. "He's supposed to ride the estate keeping trespassers away. Well, where in the hell was he last night?''

Marcus touched her cheek, catching the tear as it spilled down toward her lips. "I'm sorry,'' he said.

Aurelia bit her bottom lip to stop the trembling.

Marcus pulled her gently into his arms and held her. "It'll be okay,'' he said.

"That's a promise you can't keep,'' she said against his shoulder, crying in earnest.

"We'll figure it out, Aurelia.'' He held her and wondered if, just as before, he was giving someone false hope. "It'll be okay.'' His hand moved down her back, stroking and rubbing.

"You're the only person in this whole town who believes in me,'' Aurelia said, her face turning into his neck. "Thank you, Marcus.''

He was instantly aware of her breath on his skin, so warm and exciting. "Thanks aren't necessary. You came here to do what you had to do, Aurelia. Now you're caught in the middle of a mess. But we're putting the cart before the horse. There probably won't be any trouble.''

"You're a good man, Marcus. You care about people. Even me, a stranger."

He realized then how much he did care about Aurelia. And though he hadn't known her long, she wasn't a stranger. He'd seen qualities in her that told him who she was. She'd put her personal desires away in an attempt to do what was right for the person who depended on her. She had backbone and courage, and she was kind. What happened with Lottie Levert wasn't the only story going around town. He'd heard that she'd been kind to Joey Reynolds. That told him volumes about what kind of person she was. "You're a lot more than a stranger to me, Aurelia."

She pulled back slightly and lifted her face to stare into his eyes. "Am I?"

The invitation was there and he answered her with a kiss. Her arms lifted and went around his neck and she answered his kiss with one of her own.

Desire flooded through Marcus. Aurelia was a beautiful woman, but she was more than that. She was special. He wanted her, but it wasn't just a physical want. He wanted to protect her, to make that radiant smile rush across her face. He wanted the privilege of cherishing her. And he wanted all of those things back from her. He wanted to see her eyes light up when she saw him. Holding her in his arms and kissing her with more and more intensity, Marcus realized that he was falling in love with Aurelia. He'd denied it to himself because he knew she was leaving

Natchez. Now he accepted that he'd been fooling himself in an effort to protect his heart.

One long, passionate kiss, and he knew the truth.

Her breathing was shallow and he maneuvered her into his lap. He could feel her trembling, and he knew that apprehension was mixed with her passion. She was a young woman with limited experience. She didn't have to tell him that; he could tell. If he continued, he was taking on a grave responsibility. Yet he couldn't stop.

One arm supported her and the other began to unbutton her blouse. If he had any doubts, they vanished when her fingers began working the buttons of his shirt.

Once her shirt was open, his hand slipped under the lace of her bra. She moaned against his mouth.

Easing her onto the bed, he slowly undressed her. Morning sunlight flooded the room, yet she showed no hesitation or sign of embarrassment. She was even more beautiful than he'd dared to imagine.

When he undressed, her gaze moved up and down his body, and she smiled. She said nothing, but she lifted her arms and he joined her in the bed.

Marcus knew that nothing on earth could stop him now, and nothing could protect him. Once he began the sweet exploration of Aurelia's willing body, he was lost.

When their passion was sated, and they were clinging to each other in desperate need, he closed his eyes and dared to believe that the most incredible gift had been dropped in his arms. Cradling Aurelia against his chest, he pulled the covers over both of them.

"Are you okay?" he asked gently.

"I've never been better. Whatever that was, I want more of it," she said, her voice filled with delight. "Marcus, I've never dreamed of anything that incredible."

He pulled her more closely against his side. "I'm in danger of losing my heart, Aurelia."

There was a pause as she touched his face and turned it so that they were staring into each other's eyes. "If I'm accused of killing Lottie, will you be my lawyer?"

Marcus felt as if he'd been turned to stone. He felt nothing except panic.

"You're the only person in this town who believes in me. You're the only person I can trust. If it comes to the worst thing, will you defend me?"

Chapter Ten

"Will you?" Aurelia asked again. She saw the panic rising in him and was terrified. "Please, Marcus."

"I can't," he said. "I'll get you the best lawyer in the Southeast. If it comes to that." If he was trying to look reassuring, he was failing miserably. "Chances are that Lottie died of exposure and no one will be blamed. It'll be laid to her own foolishness."

Aurelia didn't answer. She didn't believe that and deep down, Marcus didn't either.

"What will happen next?"

"The sheriff will question you, and me, and everyone else who might be marginally involved. The coroner's report will come after that." He picked up her hand and rubbed it. Aurelia knew it was icy cold.

"And if there was foul play in Lottie's death?"

"A lot will depend on the evidence. Once the sheriff has collected all of that, he'll have to decide who he believes is guilty."

Once again Marcus stopped, but Aurelia needed to hear it all. "And then he'll arrest me."

"Believe me, there were other people with a motive to want Lottie dead."

Aurelia pulled her hand away from him. "I didn't have a motive! I didn't want her dead. Blackthorn was never hers and you know that."

Marcus grasped her shoulders. "I know it, Aurelia, but you asked me what would happen. If the evidence indicates you had something to do with Lottie's death, you'll be charged."

"And put in jail." She stated it flatly.

"Bond will be set."

"How much?" Aurelia knew she was lost. She couldn't pull together a thousand dollars, much less the bond a murder charge would require. And no one in Natchez would post a bond for her.

"It would probably be high," Marcus admitted. "You're an outsider. The risk of flight is greater."

"If I could flee from here, I would," she said in a monotone. "I'd leave right now."

"And what of Blackthorn?" Marcus asked.

Even the name sent a chill through her. "I didn't believe the legends, but now I do. Blackthorn is cursed. Andre was hung here, and it looks as if I'll be charged with a murder I didn't commit. Tell me, Marcus, in the old days, they would have hung me, wouldn't they?"

His arms went around her and pulled her against him. At first she resisted. It was only when she couldn't stop the tears that she collapsed against his shoulder and cried. "I'm so afraid. Anything can happen to me here. Please say you'll defend me," she whispered. "You're the only one who really believes I'm innocent."

"Okay," he whispered into her hair. "You have my word, Aurelia, though I think it's a foolish decision."

Aurelia shifted so she could see his face. He was as frightened as she was, yet he'd chosen to stand by her, to defy his own fear. "Thank you, Marcus. Thank you."

He brushed the tears from her cheeks. "You've accomplished what no one else could ever do, Aurelia. I haven't been in a courtroom since Wade Gammit died."

"I know." Her smile was tremulous. "But I've never been in one. And my life may well be on the line."

"Why won't you accept a more seasoned lawyer, one who has a proven track record in criminal trials?"

"Because no one else in the world will try harder for me," she said softly, her hand stroking his cheek. "I know that."

"Well," he sighed, "I suppose you're right about that part. Let's just hope that's enough."

She leaned toward him, her lips touching his. They'd just begun to kiss when there was a knock at the cottage door.

Marcus dressed hurriedly and went to answer it while Aurelia found her clothes and pulled them on.

Still barefoot, she hurried into the other room of the cottage to find Dru Colson standing there, hat in hand.

"How are you feeling, Miss Agee?" he asked.

"Okay." She shifted her weight from one foot to the other.

"Mrs. Levert's body has been removed. We should have a coroner's report soon enough."

She nodded, looking at Marcus instead of the sheriff.

"The rain last night did a lot of damage to the scene, but it would appear Mrs. Levert has been dead for several hours. There were some broken tree branches that indicated she was running through the woods for some distance."

"Can you tell how she died?" Marcus asked in a voice level and calm.

"I can't say for sure until the autopsy comes in," Dru said evasively. "Where were you last night, Miss Agee?"

"I was at Killburn for a while, but I came home about—"

"She made quite a scene at the Killburn ball," Marcus cut in smoothly. "Everyone there was talking about her."

"And when did you come home?" Dru asked.

Aurelia caught the warning look from Marcus and knew she was treading on dangerous ground. "It was late," she said. "I'm not certain. To be honest, I'm not certain of much right now."

"Did you come straight home from the ball?" Dru pressed.

In his questions, Aurelia knew he was trying to rule her in or out as a suspect in Lottie's death. She could only assume that there was enough evidence around the body to indicate Lottie's death might not be accidental.

"Yes," she said. "I came straight home and went right to bed."

Marcus was steadily watching her.

"Did you see or hear anything last night?"

"The storm was so severe, I didn't hear anything. I made a cup of herbal tea to relax me, drank it and went to bed. That's all. I never saw Lottie or even conceived she might be on Blackthorn property. She obviously drove herself. What was she doing here?"

Dru shook his head. "Looking for the mythical buried treasure, trying to frighten you, it could be any number of things."

"I've told you someone has been lurking around the cabin," Aurelia said. "I reported the broken window. Do you think it was Lottie?" She found it hard to believe that the middle-aged woman could dash through the woods throwing rocks.

Dru shook his head slightly. "I'm not ruling anything out."

"Are you ruling anything in?" Marcus asked.

Dru gave him a considering look. "Not yet. I'm collecting evidence. When I have enough of that, then

I'll begin to connect the dots and see what kind of picture I get.''

Marcus walked to Aurelia and put his arm around her shoulders. "It's been a terrible thing for Aurelia," he said. "Blackthorn's legends have upset her, and now this."

"Where was the famed highwayman when I needed him?" Aurelia asked with a halfhearted attempt at lightening the mood.

"That's a good question," Dru said. "There've been enough sightings of Andre that I'm almost willing to believe he exists—as a flesh-and-blood man on a black horse riding around the estate to try and keep the trespassers away. If I find that to be true, then he would very well be a suspect, *if* there's any need for suspects." He nodded at Aurelia and Marcus. "I'll be in touch with any new developments. Miss Agee, you're not planning on leaving any time soon, are you?"

"No, I'll be here until Blackthorn is sold."

"What are your plans there?"

"I've set up an auction for Saturday," Aurelia said, aware that it would be news to Marcus.

"I'll be in touch." The sheriff closed the door when he left.

"An auction?" Marcus asked.

"Between John Ittawasa trying to preserve the land and Lottie trying to claim it as hers, I have to sell before the entire estate is tied up in court," Aurelia said.

Marcus stared at her. "Whatever you do, don't tell anyone else that," he said slowly. "You just admitted to the perfect motive for murder."

MARCUS REMOVED the back of the big old dinosaur of a console television. Mrs. Nettie put great stock in the set, and he was careful with it. Even as he began the exploratory testing, his mind was on Aurelia.

"Hey!" He felt Dan's hands on his arms, pulling him out of the set. "Why don't you write up the receipts? I'll finish this."

Marcus didn't argue. Dan could diagnose and repair the set in half the time it would take him. It didn't hurt his ego to admit that he was only an adequate television repairman. He'd learned the danger of ego—when he'd thought he was such a hotshot lawyer.

"Are you okay?" Dan asked.

"I'm not sure," Marcus admitted. He turned to his friend and partner. "If Aurelia is charged with Lottie's murder, she's asked me to be her lawyer."

Dan put down the screwdriver he held. "I'm glad, Marcus. It's the right thing. Law has always been your real love."

"I don't want the responsibility," he said.

"The only thing you can do is your very best. I suspect that'll be good enough. What happened with Wade Gammit wasn't your fault. I don't know why you're determined to believe that it was. There was an eyewitness. There's no way the best lawyer in the world can refute a positive identification. Marvin Harrad testified in court that he saw Wade kill that 7-Eleven clerk. He said he saw him point the gun and kill her. No amount of good lawyering could have changed that guilty verdict.''

"I should have been able to shake Marvin's testimony. He was so certain it was Wade. And he was wrong.''

Dan stepped closer and put a hand on Marcus's arm. "A parade of saints couldn't have shaken Marvin's testimony. You know the old coot. Once he gets an idea in his head, there's no way to force it out. Think about what he has to live with—he's the man who put Wade in prison, not you.''

Marcus knew that Dan was correct, but it didn't alleviate the guilt. Wade Gammit was an innocent man. Marcus should have been able to prove it.

"What did kill Lottie?" Dan asked.

"The autopsy will determine that,'' Marcus said. "I'm hoping for exposure.''

"She was a dingbat,'' Dan said. "There was no telling what she'd do at any given time. Do you think she was up at Blackthorn to try and scare Aurelia away?''

"It's very possible. Like you say, Lottie was capable of almost anything.''

"Well, I hope Miss Agee isn't charged with anything. That would be the proper outcome. But if she is, she'll have the best lawyer in Mississippi.''

"If only that were true,'' Marcus said. He picked

up the account book and settled in at the big desk in the corner. If he wasn't the greatest at repairs, he was excellent at keeping the books.

AURELIA SELF-CONSCIOUSLY took a seat at the counter at Ella's. She gratefully took the cup of coffee the older woman set before her.

"I heard about Lottie," Ella said. "That's too bad. She was one of the town characters. Looks like she finally pushed the boundaries of her luck."

"Ella, you said you saw red and blue flashing lights at Blackthorn woods. Was it this?"

Ella took a seat on the stool beside her. There were only a few customers in the diner and other waitresses were taking care of them. "I'd say that would be it. It's hard for me to know."

"I fainted," Aurelia admitted. "Marcus carried me to the cottage. I didn't really see any flashing lights, but that would have been when the ambulance came."

Ella nodded.

"Did you see anything else?" Aurelia asked, her heart tripping rapidly.

"The images are very fast," Ella explained. "Sometimes I don't understand them at all. I don't remember anything except the flashing lights and you and Marcus standing together. That's how I knew both of you were okay."

"Am I okay?" Aurelia asked, embarrassed that she was about to cry.

"You are," Ella said. "And so is Marcus. You have to understand that things happen for a reason."

"I can't see the reason behind this," Aurelia said.

"Oh, but there is one. I can guarantee that."

There was something so positive in Ella's voice that Aurelia put her coffee cup down. "What do you know?"

Ella shook her head. "Nothing."

"What have you seen?" She knew she had to ask the right question.

"Marcus has been on my mind again. I saw him standing outside a blue building. There was a sign, and he was smiling." She shrugged.

"Did you recognize the building?"

"You're a very good investigator," Ella said. "I did. It was his old law building."

"And the sign?"

"He was hanging out his shingle again. He was practicing law again."

Aurelia felt her stomach drop. The only way Marcus would ever take up the law again would be if he was defending her.

"Marcus is a fine lawyer. He should practice again," Ella said. "I feel you played a role in that decision."

"I did," Aurelia said in a flat voice. "If he's practicing law again, he's defending me against a murder charge."

MARCUS WAS STILL bent over the books when a shadow fell across the balance sheet.

"A computer would be so much faster," Dru said.

"It would require giving up my ledgers," Marcus said carefully.

"Am I correct in assuming you're going to serve as Aurelia's lawyer?"

Marcus felt the pain like a physical blow. "Is Aurelia going to need a lawyer?"

"Could be," Dru said. "Lottie's death wasn't accidental."

"You're sure of that?"

"Very sure. There were ligature marks on Lottie's throat and a scalp contusion to the back of her head. It appears she was hit from behind and then strangled."

There was no way the death would be ruled accidental. Someone had killed Lottie, but Marcus knew it wasn't Aurelia. "Can you tell me who your suspects are?" he asked.

Dru shook his head. "I'll be filing a report. You can read it when I finish. I have to say Aurelia is right at the top of the list of suspects, though. Convince her not to do anything foolish."

"I will," Marcus promised. He watched Dru walk out of the shop and into a sunny February morning. After the cold, torrential rain, spring had come calling in Natchez.

"I couldn't help but overhear," Dan said. "Is he going to arrest Miss Agee?"

"Probably," Marcus said.

"Forget about the books. I'll do them after I close

up today. You'd better get busy planning your defense.''

Marcus couldn't help but smile at the eagerness in his partner's face. "So, you think the business will run better if I go back to law?''

"Maybe just a little,'' Dan said, clapping him on the shoulder. "You're a far better lawyer and you know it.''

"I need to talk to Aurelia. She's going to take this mighty hard.''

"You tell her not everyone in Natchez believes she's guilty.''

"I will.'' Marcus gathered his things and left.

THE DRIVE TO Blackthorn had never been more beautiful. It seemed that the cold rain and the first hours of hot sun had brought the plants to life. Aurelia was amazed that some things were already budding. It was mid-February, but spring was just around the corner.

She slowed when she saw the expensive SUV parked in front of the caretaker's cottage. Leon Kimball was sitting on a rocker on her porch. He rose when she got out of her car and walked toward him.

"I heard about the auction,'' he said. "Not a good idea. Especially not now, with another dead body on Blackthorn.''

"Thanks for the opinion,'' Aurelia said.

"It's more than an opinion. I've come to make a cash offer, right this minute. You can have the money within an hour and you can be gone from here.''

"I don't need to run," Aurelia said, though it sounded like the smartest move she could make.

"Lots of innocent people go to jail," Leon said. "Ask Marcus, he's real familiar with that scenario."

He was scaring her, but she was determined not to show it. "That won't happen. I didn't hurt Lottie."

"My offer is four hundred thousand, cash."

"But you offered half a million two days ago." Aurelia knew she sounded frantic and she hated it.

"Blackthorn is cursed. That drops the price." Leon grinned. "What about it, Aurelia? Sign the deed, go by the bank and get the cash, and then drive yourself out of town. Once you're gone, all of this will blow over."

Aurelia was naive, but she wasn't stupid. "Somehow, I don't think Sheriff Colson will just forget Lottie Levert was found dead on Blackthorn property."

"Maybe, maybe not. Are you willing to risk hanging around and maybe getting charged with murder?" He reached into the pocket of his jacket and pulled out a check. "Take it."

Aurelia walked past him and unlocked the cottage door. "No thanks, Leon. I don't think that would be very smart. If someone did kill Lottie and I took your offer, it might look as if I were trying to flee."

He shook his head. "It only works in my favor, Aurelia. Every day the value of this place drops. By Saturday, I'll buy it for three hundred thousand. Or very possibly, less."

"You are despicable." Aurelia started to slam the door in his face, but his hand caught it.

"I'm trying to help you. If you're charged with Lottie's murder, Randall will have legal grounds to stop you from selling Blackthorn. He can tie the estate up for years. Don't you see that?"

"And you're so very noble, you've dropped your original offer by a hundred thousand dollars just so you can capitalize on my problems."

Leon smiled. "I'm trying to help you, but I'm not an idiot. Why should I pay more than I have to?"

"No, you're not an idiot," Aurelia said. "But it remains to be seen what you truly are."

She slammed the door and slid the bolt home. It was only when she tried to walk to the faucet for some water that she realized how weak and afraid she really was.

Chapter Eleven

Marcus sat in Dru Colson's office and tried not to eavesdrop so obviously as the sheriff spoke to one of his officers on the phone. "Have the car checked thoroughly," Dru said.

The sheriff had to be talking about Lottie Levert's car, Marcus thought. Dru Colson was taking his investigation of Lottie's death step by step. Marcus could only hope that there was evidence that someone else was with Lottie on the night she was killed.

When Dru hung up, he turned his attention to Marcus. "The coroner is putting Lottie's time of death between midnight and four this morning. When did Aurelia leave the dance?" he asked.

Marcus hesitated. Dru Colson was a good man and a good sheriff, but now his job was in conflict with Marcus's goal—to protect Aurelia's future. But in so doing, he was ethically bound not to lie. "I can't be positive," he answered, which wasn't a lie. He hadn't seen Aurelia leave the party.

"Amy Wintzel says she left around eleven."

Marcus figured the sheriff would find witnesses; he just hadn't expected the lawman to work that fast. "That's possible," he admitted. Then countered with, "Is Aurelia strong enough to make the marks on Lottie's neck? Lottie wasn't an invalid. She would have fought back."

"Not if she was knocked unconscious. Or almost unconscious."

It was a good point, and one that wouldn't go in Aurelia's favor.

"As soon as you get the complete autopsy, I'd like to see it," Marcus said.

"I'll give you a call."

"And your report."

"That, too," Dru said. He hesitated. "I just want to tell you, Marcus, that I'm sorry all of this has happened. I know Miss Agee is in a difficult spot. There's no telling what Lottie was doing up at Blackthorn. But if there's any chance that this was self-defense, Miss Agee should say so now."

Marcus nodded. "If that was the case, I believe Aurelia would have said so."

Dru stood up. "I'll call you when all the reports are in."

"Do you expect to charge anyone immediately?"

"I have no plans until I examine all the evidence," Dru promised, "and I hope as much as you that it doesn't point to the heiress of Blackthorn."

"Thanks, Dru." He knew the sheriff meant every word he'd spoken.

"Miss Agee isn't planning on leaving Natchez, is she?" Dru asked.

Marcus shook his head. "She intends on selling the estate, but she has no plans to leave."

Dru hesitated. "It might be best if Miss Agee postponed the auction." He held up a hand at the protest that Marcus started to make. "Think about it, Marcus."

"If she isn't charged—"

"Legally, I can't stop you at this time. As a friend, I'm telling you it would be best if she didn't take any rash actions."

Marcus considered what the sheriff had said. He nodded. "I see your point, Dru, but I don't think Aurelia will. She's determined to sell Blackthorn, and the sooner the better is the way she's looking at it. There are pressing family obligations."

AURELIA MADE another cup of tea. The last two had grown cold because she'd forgotten them. The long day was finally winding down. She'd waited all afternoon for word from Marcus, but none had come.

She sipped the tea as she continued pacing the small cottage. When she had emptied the cup, she sat down in a chair and put on her hiking boots. She needed a long walk. She was going to go crazy if she didn't get out of the small cottage.

What might have been another lovely sunset was

blocked by a mass of heavy gray clouds on the western horizon. She'd learned already that storms most often moved from west to east across the river town. And there seemed to be plenty of storms. It felt as if days had passed since she'd seen the sun. But that, in all probability, was just her bad mood.

She headed up the path to the old pillars and the big burial mound. It was probably sacrilegious, but she wanted to climb to the top of it. As she edged around the wicked-looking thicket of devil's walking sticks, she wondered about the plants. Had they been deliberately planted, or had they simple grown up and taken over? Probably the latter, but there was no way to tell for certain. She hadn't noticed it before, but a narrow path wound through the thicket.

She hesitated, then walked on to the burial mound. She'd save the thorn tree thicket for another exploration. The mound was steeper than she remembered, and it was only with some difficulty that she climbed to the top. To her surprise, she discovered that it flattened on top, plateaulike. Standing on the large, flat surface, she had a terrific view. She could see the old pillars of the estate as well as the shell-covered path and the caretaker's cottage. The top of the mound made a perfect lookout.

As she walked along she was struck by the thick grass and the lack of trees. It looked as if someone had tended the mound, keeping it free of trash trees and brambles. But who?

She'd ask that of Marcus and the sheriff. While

Blackthorn was private property, it didn't seem to keep many people out. Lottie was a perfect example. What had the woman been doing in the Blackthorn woods? And who had hurt her? Aurelia felt a chill as the many legends of Blackthorn came back to her.

She walked to the farthest edge of the mound and stared into the thick trees of the forest. Not even the advantage of height gave her a clear view. The trees crowded together. Anyone—or anything—could be hiding in the woods. Waiting.

A cold wind cut across the mound, and Aurelia shivered more deeply into her coat. Dusk fell swiftly in winter and it was time to go back to the cottage. Maybe Marcus had called and when she didn't answer, he might be on his way.

Cheered at that thought, she carefully began the descent. She was halfway down when she heard the sound of a baby crying. The plaintive wail seemed caught in the wind that swept over the estate. Though she listened intently, Aurelia couldn't tell where the sound was coming from. She only knew that it was the saddest sound she'd ever heard.

Spurred to action, she nearly tripped as she tried to run down the steep incline. She caught herself at the bottom and regained her balance. Panting, she listened. The baby had stopped crying. But as soon as she started walking, the helpless cry began again.

The cry was so real and so distressed that Aurelia felt the goose bumps march over her back and arms. Whatever was happening, there was one very un-

happy infant somewhere on the property. If this was
no ghost, then some adult had brought the baby onto
the property. And left it? The very idea made Aurelia
upset. If the child had been abandoned, it would be
cold. Left unattended, an infant wouldn't last long in
the February storm that was brewing. But what if this
was no human infant? What if this was the baby Marcus had spoken of? She had to find out. She couldn't
risk abandoning a living child.

Determined to find the infant, Aurelia remembered
the path through the thorn trees. That sounded like
the direction the crying originated from.

Wishing she'd thought to bring a flashlight, Aurelia
set off through the thicket in the fading light. The
baby's cry seemed to guide her, but she couldn't be
certain. At times it sounded near, then it would fade.

Darkness deepened with each passing moment.
Without a light the path became indiscernible. It
twisted and turned through the cruel trees, disappearing at times. Aurelia continued to stumble forward,
guided by the mournful cry of the infant.

After fifteen minutes, she realized that she was getting no closer to the crying child. The sound was like
a phantom crying. It shifted on the wind, coming from
the north, then the west, leading her in circles.

Her thoughts returned to the story of the ghostly
infant. She'd seen the horse and rider. She hadn't believed it was a ghost, but now she couldn't shake the
idea that Blackthorn was haunted, and by more than
one unhappy ghost. It was easier to admit it in the

gathering night. Perhaps the spirits of those who remained wanted no interference from her.

She knew she was scaring herself, but she couldn't stop the thoughts that whirled in her mind. Since coming to Blackthorn, her life had become a tangle. In Minneapolis, life had been simple and straightforward. She'd done her duty, cared for her mother and awakened each morning knowing exactly what the day would bring.

At Blackthorn, anything was possible. Trespassers, the touch of Marcus's lips on hers, the unexpected sense of someone to count on, a dead body in the woods—and a ghost. If Andre Agee rode the woods of Blackthorn on Diable, why not a lost infant spirit crying for help?

The rules of life she'd learned in Minneapolis didn't count at Blackthorn. She'd been foolish to think they would. One thing was certain, though: if this crying baby was flesh and blood, she would find it.

The baby's crying picked up in volume, and Aurelia slipped deeper into the thicket. She'd lost the path completely, and she wasn't certain she could find her way out. Her breath caught in her lungs as she realized she was lost.

A bitter wind picked up as she turned slowly in a circle. The path had disappeared. The sound of the crying baby had stopped. She stood alone in the thicket without a clue to the direction she needed to go to find her way out.

It was almost as if she'd been led and then abandoned. Fear coursed through her as her limbs began
to tremble.

Turning slowly, she tried to get her bearings, but
it did no good. The thorn trees crowded in on her in
all directions. Total darkness had fallen, and the sky
was too cloudy to allow a glimmer of moonlight.

Reaching a hand out, she felt the thorns in all directions. She was totally lost. She'd have to spend the
night in the thicket and hope that it didn't rain.

She was about to give in to her fear when she heard
the sound of galloping hooves. Aurelia felt a surge of
fear—Andre had returned again. Was it possible that
this time he meant to banish all trespassers, including
her? She'd come to sell his estate. In all likelihood,
this land that he had once loved would be turned into
a commercial venture. If his ghost did patrol the
grounds of Blackthorn, it would certainly object to
that.

As the sound of the galloping horse drew closer,
Aurelia took a shaky breath. If it was time to confront
Andre, so be it. Anything was better than the dread
that had crept into her heart.

"Aurelia!"

She recognized Marcus's voice. He was the one
riding on the estate, and he was hunting for her.

"Marcus!" she called. "I'm in the thicket. Keep
talking." She felt her fear turn to a strange kind of
exhilaration. She began to move in the direction of
his voice.

"Aurelia!"

"I'm coming," she said, hurrying toward his voice.

"What in heaven's name are you doing in there?" Marcus called to her, guiding her with his voice.

Aurelia admitted her own foolishness. "I heard the baby crying. It sounded like it was coming from here."

"There's no baby at Blackthorn," Marcus said.

"Perhaps you're right," Aurelia agreed. She'd searched, but she hadn't found a baby. But she'd heard one crying. There was no doubt of that.

To her delight, she saw a glimmer of light that could come only from a flashlight. She moved toward it through the last of the thorn trees, carefully avoiding the long thorns of the trees. When at last she broke out of the thicket, she couldn't hide her happiness in seeing Marcus astride Cogar.

"Thank goodness you decided to ride this way," she said.

"I came deliberately. The horses needed some exercise, so I rode over to check on you. When your car was at the cottage and you weren't, I waited. Then I became concerned."

"It's a good thing you did," Aurelia said, walking up to pat the big gray's neck. "I was lost. I followed that crying baby into the thicket, and then the crying stopped."

Marcus held his hand down. "Hop up," he said, kicking the stirrup free for her to use.

In a moment, Aurelia was mounted behind him, her

body snug against his strong back. It was such a luxury to wrap her arms around him that she closed her eyes. Cogar kept a sedate walk as they headed toward the cottage.

''I heard the horse's hooves and I thought it was Andre, coming to finish me off,'' Aurelia said, her hands spread across his chest. ''But it was you, coming to rescue me.''

''Andre would have no reason to harm you,'' Marcus said. ''You're his flesh and blood, the heir to Blackthorn.''

''Maybe Andre doesn't want the estate sold,'' she said, musing as she held on to the comfort of his strong body.

''Even so, I doubt he'd hurt you.'' One of his hands moved up to hold hers against his chest. ''Andre would never hurt you,'' he repeated.

''Do you ride on the estate often?'' Aurelia asked.

''I used to. Before you came. Lately I've been riding on some property to the east of Blackthorn.''

''Have you ever heard the baby crying?'' Aurelia asked.

''No, I haven't. But I'm very curious about this crying infant. Lots of people have reported seeing Andre and Diable, but until you moved onto the estate, no one except Yvonne heard the crying baby for decades.''

''Lucky me,'' Aurelia said.

Marcus stopped Cogar. ''I don't think either of us

has had much luck lately, Aurelia, and I think that we're about to hit another streak of bad.''

"Why?'' she asked. When he didn't answer, she leaned around him to see Sheriff Dru Colson standing in front of her cottage.

"COULDN'T THIS WAIT until morning?'' Marcus asked the sheriff as Dru waited for Aurelia to unlock the cottage door.

"I wish it could wait, but I need to look around,'' Dru said.

"For what?'' Marcus asked.

"Miss Agee, I'd like a sample of your hair, if you wouldn't mind.''

"You're going to need a warrant—'' Marcus started.

"No, it's okay. I don't have anything to hide,'' Aurelia said. "He can have it.'' She pushed the door open. "Come inside, Sheriff.''

The three of them stepped inside, and Aurelia realized how cold she'd been. Before she did anything else, she put more logs on the fire in the fireplace and put the kettle on for a pot of coffee. She felt as if she'd stepped into a dream—someone else's.

"I'm sorry,'' Dru said, looking first at Marcus and then at Aurelia. "I'd rather have waited until morning, but the quicker I do this, the sooner all of this will be over. If I could get that hair sample, I'll be on my way.''

Aurelia frowned. "Do you need to cut it?''

Dru shook his head. "If you have a brush or comb, that would be fine."

"Of course." Aurelia stepped past the men and went into the bathroom. She kept a brush on the vanity. Flipping on the light, she stared at the empty countertop. There was a drawer so she opened it. It was empty except for the nail polish she'd bought for the ball.

She knelt and looked through the cabinet where several towels and washcloths were folded. There was no sign of the brush.

Confused, she walked back to the room where both men were waiting for her. "My brush is missing," she said, walking to her handbag. She dumped all the contents on the kitchen table. The brush wasn't there, but she picked up a comb. Several strands of her dark hair were tangled around the teeth.

"Is anything else missing?" Dru asked.

"I haven't noticed anything." Aurelia was puzzled.

"Check through the cottage," Dru said, depositing the comb in a plastic bag he pulled from his jacket pocket.

"I can't imagine where the brush got off to," she said, frowning. "I don't have anything of value here. It doesn't make sense that someone would steal a brush."

"I'm sorry to trouble you," Dru said as he opened the door and stepped onto the porch. "I'll be in touch."

"I'm sure he will," Marcus said as he stepped forward to latch the door. "They must have found some hair on Lottie's body. They're trying to make a match."

"I didn't touch her," Aurelia said. "It's okay."

Marcus walked to her and put both hands on her shoulders. "I'm not so sure about that, Aurelia. How long has your brush been missing?"

Chapter Twelve

Marcus held Aurelia close against him. They were both fully clothed, exhausted by the possibilities of what the next day might bring. At last Aurelia had given in to her exhaustion and slept, but sleep escaped Marcus. He was too worried. After he'd taken Cogar back to his stables, he'd stayed at Aurelia's side.

He'd tried his best not to let Aurelia see how upset he was by the sheriff's request for a hair sample and by the missing brush. He could predict exactly what the next turn of events would be: Aurelia's hair would match the hair found on Lottie Levert. Aurelia would be charged with murder. He knew the sequence of events because it was the stuff of his worst nightmares—someone he loved dependent on his skills to save her. In the nightmare, he never saw the outcome because anxiety woke him up. But he didn't have to dream the ending; he already knew what it felt like to know that an innocent person was wrongly convicted because of his inadequacies.

Marcus felt Aurelia stir. She mumbled something indistinguishable against his shoulder. He shifted so that she rested on his arm, her face turned up slightly so that he could see the frown that marred her beautiful features. Even in her sleep there was no rest. She struggled briefly, then fell back into a sound sleep.

Marcus stroked her face, easing a dark curl off her cheek. Her skin was flawless, her eyelashes a dark fan against her smooth cheek. Her full lips were tinted red, slightly pursed as she slept. She was incredibly beautiful, and totally vulnerable. She'd put her trust in him and his ability to protect her. The thought made his stomach knot with anxiety.

If only he'd followed her when she left the ball. If only Andre and Diable had been guarding the grounds of Blackthorn on the night Lottie decided to trespass. There were a lot of things Marcus would change if he could. If only he hadn't agreed to represent Aurelia. That was the biggest one. She deserved the best lawyer she could find.

Once the charge was made against her, perhaps he could convince her to hire a more experienced trial lawyer. Somehow, though, he doubted it. She was one stubborn woman.

He shifted and she turned with him, curling into his body in a way that pierced his heart. She was a grown woman, but in many ways she was still naive. She had no idea how awry the justice system could go.

He was still holding her when the sun broke the horizon and slowly rose in the sky. The storm had passed without rain, and the new day would be clear and cold. He was staring down at her when she opened her eyes.

"You didn't sleep at all, did you?" she asked, her hand shifting to his face to trace the lines beneath his eyes.

"Some," he fibbed, not wanting to worry her.

"I had a dream," she said softly. "I was riding behind a masked man on a big black horse." She smiled. "It must have been because of last night, the way I was riding behind you, because I felt safe with this man."

"Maybe it was the future," he said, wanting to tease her until she smiled again.

"You think I'm going to take up with Andre and his horse?" she asked.

"That would be the perfect ending to this story," Marcus said, kissing her on the nose so that she couldn't see the pain in his eyes. If only Andre could save her, but the ghost rider was powerless against the forces of the law.

"Is there anything you especially wanted to do in Natchez?" he asked. He had the terrible feeling that Aurelia's days of freedom were limited.

"Yes," she said. "I'd like to ride again."

"Perfect," he said, tossing back the quilt that he'd pulled over them during the night. "Let's do it."

AURELIA FELT much more secure on Mariah's back than she had the first time she'd ridden. As she led the way into the forest, she urged the mare into a trot. Marcus had taught her how to post, but her muscles weren't totally cooperative. She took a few hard bounces and then caught the rhythm of the trot. She was moving in unison with Mariah. She turned and gave Marcus a big smile.

"You're a natural," he said as his horse trotted beside her. "If you had a few weeks to ride every day, you'd become a very good rider."

"I'd like that," she said. "Growing up in a city, horseback riding lessons were too expensive. But I always wanted to learn." She ducked a low-hanging limb and laughed. "I wanted to be a cowgirl, but somehow I don't think cowgirls ride in these little English saddles."

"Next time we'll try Western," he promised.

Marcus's pleasure in her happiness was almost more than Aurelia could take. No one in her whole adult life had ever bothered to ask what made her happy. Unexpectedly, she felt the pressure of tears. Boldly, she urged Mariah to canter.

"That's the way to ride," Marcus called encouragement from behind. He hung back and allowed her to take the lead, setting the pace.

The ride was thrilling. Aurelia let Mariah gallop until the horse slowed of her own accord. She checked her watch, surprised to see that she'd been riding for over an hour. She pulled Mariah to a walk, listening to the sound of Cogar's pounding hooves as he caught up.

"I'm impressed," Marcus said. "I'm also afraid your thighs are going to feel this tomorrow."

Aurelia shook her head. "I can't worry about tomorrow," she said, realizing that for the first time in her life she could say that and mean it. "I'm too happy right this moment to let the past or the future interfere."

"I'll give Mariah some extra carrots. She's certainly worked a miracle on you."

Aurelia reached over and touched his thigh. "It's not just Mariah or the ride. It's you. Thank you, Marcus." She was about to withdraw her hand when she saw Marcus's expression change. Worry furrowed his brow.

They'd just rounded the bend that gave them a view of the cottage. The sheriff's car was parked beside her rental car. As the horses walked toward the cottage, Dru got out of the patrol car.

Aurelia could tell he'd brought bad news. She lifted the reins and stopped Mariah.

"Sheriff," she said.

"Miss Agee, I need for you to come into town with me."

"Dru," Marcus said, vaulting off the horse. "I'll bring her in. Let us put the horses away."

Dru shook his head. "I'm sorry, Marcus. She'll have to come with me now."

Aurelia dismounted. Reins in her hand, she walked forward. "What is it?"

"We found several hairs clutched in Lottie's right hand. They matched the hair we took from your comb."

"I wasn't anywhere near Mrs. Levert," Aurelia said calmly. Her heart was pounding, but she simply had to make the sheriff understand. "Someone stole my brush. Remember? I told you last night."

"I'll be glad to take a statement at the courthouse," Dru said as he walked to Aurelia and removed the reins from her hand and gave them to Marcus. He gently began to move Aurelia toward the patrol car.

"Don't say anything else, Aurelia," Marcus said, stepping in front of the sheriff. "Don't ask her any more questions, Dru. Not without her attorney present."

"But I don't have anything to hide," Aurelia insisted.

Marcus blocked their path. "Aurelia, promise me you won't say another word."

"I promise," she said reluctantly. She was upset, but Marcus was far more troubled than she was. This was a misunderstanding.

"I'll be there as soon as I can," Marcus said as he watched the sheriff put her in the back of the patrol car.

She stared out the window as she drove past Marcus. He leaped onto Cogar's back and set off at a gallop. Mariah was running beside him. Turning so she could watch him from the rear window of the car, Aurelia lifted a hand in a goodbye wave though she knew he couldn't sec it.

MARCUS UNSADDLED and turned the horses free in the pasture before he jumped in his truck and drove to the courthouse. He found Aurelia in an interview room with a cup of hot coffee. She was alone, and when he walked through the door, her face lit with relief.

"They haven't asked me any questions," she said.

"Good," Marcus said. He had to figure out a way to make Aurelia understand that even simple things could be turned against her. Dru was an honorable man, but if the evidence pointed at Aurelia, then he would present the case against her.

"I was thinking about the brush," Aurelia said, tapping her fingers on the lone table in the room. "When I got home from the ball, the cottage door was unlocked. Someone must have come in and taken the brush then."

He put his hands on her shoulders. "Did you notice anything else missing?" he asked.

She shook her head. "I didn't bring anything but my clothes and a few cosmetics. If something else was taken from the cottage, I wouldn't be able to tell."

The door of the interview room opened and Dru stepped inside. "Are you ready to answer some questions?" he asked.

"Yes," Aurelia said quickly. She looked up at Marcus. "We're ready, aren't we? We just have to explain that I didn't have anything to do with Lottie's death."

Dru motioned Marcus into a chair as he took the one across the table from Aurelia. "Mrs. Levert filed a statement that you'd threatened her. Tell me what happened in front of the church."

Aurelia recounted the incident, giving Dru the name of the woman who'd witnessed the incident.

"Randall said that you threatened him at the Kill-burn Ball and that you made additional threats against his mother. What happened?"

"He said I threatened him?" Aurelia looked over at Marcus. "That's a lie. I never—"

"What happened?" Dru asked.

"We were dancing and I told him I was going to sell Blackthorn. He became very upset. I walked away."

"You didn't threaten him?" Dru pressed.

"Of course not. What would I threaten him with?" Aurelia asked. "I doubt I could hurt him even if I wanted to."

Marcus rose abruptly. "What did Randall say?" he asked Dru.

Dru ignored his question. "Did you threaten his mother?"

"I didn't threaten anyone," Aurelia said. "I'm not the kind of person who issues threats. I told Randall I was selling Blackthorn and that he had no right to try and stop me. If their claim to Blackthorn was legitimate, they would have taken legal steps long before now.''

"Did Randall say he was going to stop you?" Dru asked.

"He said—"

"Aurelia," Marcus interrupted. "We need to talk, privately."

She stopped. "No matter what I say, it's going to look like I had a reason to harm Mrs. Levert. But I didn't. She had no real claim to Blackthorn. She wasn't a threat, and even though Randall got upset with me, he isn't a threat, either. I had no reason to want to hurt either of them.''

Dru stood up and stepped out the door. "Marcus, could I talk to you?" he asked.

Marcus followed him outside the room. The sheriff closed the door. "I'm going to have to charge her," he said. "Lottie Levert was murdered. Aurelia had opportunity and motive. I have physical evidence that puts her at the scene of the murder.''

"You can't be serious," Marcus said. "Lottie had no real claim to Blackthorn and you know it.''

"Lottie's claim was never proven or disproved. I believe she intended to stop the sale of Blackthorn. Whether she had just claim or not, an injunction could have seriously delayed the sale of the property.''

"And you think Aurelia was so impatient that she killed Lottie to get her out of the way?''

Dru frowned. "The little I've been around Aurelia,

I have to say that doesn't sound like her. But that's what a jury will decide, Marcus. Guilt or innocence isn't my job.''

''You can't charge her with murder if you don't believe she did it.''

''Someone killed Lottie. I know that for sure. I'm sorry that the evidence points at Aurelia, but it does.'' Dru opened the door to the interview room and stepped back inside.

''Miss Agee, I'm charging you with the murder of Lottie Levert,'' he said.

''What?'' Aurelia half rose from her chair, then stumbled back into it. She looked past the sheriff and into Marcus's eyes. ''This can't be happening,'' she said.

Marcus held her gaze with his. ''It's going to be okay,'' he promised her. ''This is just a mistake.''

AURELIA SAT in the cell. The bond hearing was scheduled for ten o'clock, and after one night in jail, she was desperate to get out. Marcus had spent as much time with her as possible, but he couldn't spend every minute there.

He'd prepared her for a bond of at least a hundred thousand dollars. Coming up with the percentage necessary to make bond was mind-boggling. And Aurelia was worried about her mother. She'd never left her for so long, and even though she was in a high-quality care facility, Aurelia believed her daily visits comforted her mother.

Pacing the cell, Aurelia halted when she heard the clang of the door that led to the jail. She looked up to find Leon Kimball headed her way.

"Miss Agee," he said, stopping in front of her cell. "My mind can hardly take in this turn of events."

Aurelia didn't bother responding.

"How are you?" he asked.

"What do you want?" Aurelia asked him. She had no desire to banter with the man.

"I've come with a little proposition," Leon said, leaning closer to the bars so he could lower his voice. "I've got a backdated bill of sale. If you sign it, no one will be able to stop the sale of Blackthorn."

"I don't think that would be in my best interest," Aurelia said.

"Oh, I disagree," Leon said softly. "Randall Levert has hired a lawyer to file an injunction stopping the sale of Blackthorn. He has the sympathy of the community behind him now, Miss Agee. Your only chance of disposing of that property in the next two years is to sell it to me now."

Aurelia's hands were clenched into fists at her sides. "All my life I've tried to do the right thing," Aurelia said. "I always believed that if I treated people fairly, I would be treated fairly in return. I see that doesn't apply here in Natchez. Why don't you just pull out a gun and point it at me, Mr. Kimball? What you're doing is exactly the same thing. You're trying to threaten and intimidate me into selling my mother's estate. Well, it won't work." She turned her back on him.

"Miss Agee," Leon said in a contrite voice. "I owe you an apology. I've been trying to help you in my own way, but I see how it must look to you."

Aurelia turned back to face him and was surprised at the expression on his face.

"I have been rather heavy-handed," he said. "I want Blackthorn, and I fear that Randall will tie it up in court. I honestly believe that may happen. But I can see how it would seem that I'm trying to force you into a decision. Listen, you have my word on the price. I'll go back to a half million dollars, as I originally offered. And that stands firm for the next six months."

Aurelia stepped closer to see if she could read his face. "Good for six months even if I go ahead with the auction?"

He nodded. "The property is worth that. I can stand firm behind that offer, no matter how you try to sell it."

"Thank you, Mr. Kimball," Aurelia said. "That takes a load off my mind."

"Good," he said, smiling at her. "I realize this hasn't been a picnic for you. All you've been trying to do is sell the property and get a good price for your mother. I'm sure Sheriff Colson will figure out who actually killed Lottie and you'll be out of here in no time."

"I hope that's true," Aurelia said, unable to hide

the dismay in her voice. "I have no idea what happened to Mrs. Levert. All I know is that I didn't harm her."

"I'm sure it will work out fine," Leon said.

There was the sound of the jail door opening again and a frown crossed Leon's face. "I'll be on my way, Miss Agee," he said, walking away from her cell.

"Hello, Mr. Kimball," Joey Reynolds said as he passed the developer. "Miss Agee," Joey said sadly. "I heard you were in jail. I know you didn't do anything wrong."

Aurelia was touched by Joey's concern. "Thanks for coming to see me."

"I told the sheriff he should let you out of jail, that you were a nice person." Joey's face fell. "He said he couldn't right now. Maybe later."

"Thank you for telling him that, Joey. Are you okay?"

"I want to go to Blackthorn, but Mrs. Harris said I shouldn't."

"Yvonne Harris?"

Joey nodded. "She fixed it so I could live at the church. She's a nice lady, too."

"She's right, Joey. You should stay away from Blackthorn for a little while."

"Mrs. Levert was killed there," Joey said solemnly. "But you didn't hurt her."

"No, I didn't."

"She was sneaking around up there. That was wrong."

"She was trespassing," Aurelia agreed.

"She saw something she shouldn't have seen."

Aurelia looked at Joey. "What do you mean?"

"She was sneaking around. She saw something but then someone saw her watching."

Chill bumps slipped up Aurelia's arms. "What did Lottie see, Joey? Do you know?"

"She was looking for the treasure, but Andre didn't want her to have it."

Aurelia's hopes dropped. Joey was weaving Lottie's death into the lore of Blackthorn. For a brief moment she'd hoped that somehow Joey had heard or seen something that might help prove who actually killed Lottie.

"Andre doesn't like people sneaking around," Joey continued. "Especially not nosy people like Mrs. Levert."

There was the sound of someone coming into the jail, and in a moment one of the deputies unlocked her cell door. "It's time for the bond hearing, Miss Agee," he said. "Your lawyer is waiting in the courtroom."

"Will you be here tomorrow?" Joey asked.

"I hope not," Aurelia said.

"If you're home, can I come to Blackthorn?"

"Sure." Aurelia felt the deputy's hand on her arm as he prepared to escort her to the courtroom. "Call before you come, Joey," she said, "and promise you won't go out to Blackthorn unless I'm there."

"I promise," Joey said. "I'll call you."

Chapter Thirteen

"Bond is set at one hundred thousand dollars," Judge Orville Brown said, not unkindly.

"Don't worry," Marcus whispered softly to her. "Since Blackthorn is the alleged motive in Lottie's death, Ella is going to make a property bond."

"She is?" Aurelia was amazed. "Why? She hardly knows me."

"But she knows me," Marcus said. "And what little she knows of you, she likes." He squeezed her shoulder. "There are some nice people in Natchez," he said.

"I know at least one," Aurelia answered, looking deep into his eyes. "Two if we count Ella."

"I've talked with Freddie Morgan. He's a fine lawyer. He's willing to take your case."

Aurelia took a deep breath. "Don't do this to me. I want you to defend me." She'd put her trust in Marcus. Never before in her life had she felt so certain of a man's goodness. In every way, he'd shown her that he respected her needs and wishes, even if they went against his own.

Marcus shook his head. "All night I thought about this. Wade Gammit would be alive if he'd had another lawyer. I can't risk this. Not with you."

He didn't have to touch her to communicate his feelings. Aurelia felt how much he cared about her.

"You've become the most important thing in my life," he said.

"I have great faith in you. Have some in yourself," Aurelia whispered softly. "I need you to do this, Marcus. For both of us." She put a hand on his arm. "You gave me your word."

"Aurelia," he said, shaking his head. "I won't fight you. Not on this. Okay, I'll do what you ask."

She squeezed his arm. "If you can't have total faith in yourself, then believe in me and what I see in you."

Aurelia knew that she'd won her point, and now it was time to change the subject. "I may have misjudged Leon Kimball. He stopped by the jail and returned to his original offer of half a million for Blackthorn. He said he realized I was in a tight spot and that the offer was good for the next six months."

Marcus's eyebrows lifted. "That's the most decent thing I've heard of Leon doing. I'm impressed. I know how badly he wants the Blackthorn property. Perhaps he's hoping this gesture will win you over about selling to him. And he's still getting Blackthorn at a rock-bottom price."

"The good thing is that it takes the heat off me to sell this instant, especially since you got an extension on the taxes. But I still need to sell and get back to Mother. She has no one else."

"One thing at a time, Aurelia. Dru suggested that you hold off on the sale of Blackthorn. I'm afraid he's right."

"I know," Aurelia said. "So what are we going to do to prove that I'm innocent?"

"Since you don't have an alibi, we're going to have to figure out who actually killed Lottie."

Aurelia sighed. "That's a pretty tall order. I never considered myself to be a sleuth."

"I've got Dru's initial reports. We'll go over them after we get out of the courthouse."

Aurelia looked around, knowing that the courtroom was going to be her second home for the duration of the trial. It was a pretty bleak prospect. In a week's time, her life had been altered so radically that she had difficulty grasping what had happened. "Let's get out of here."

MARCUS SAT AT the small table in the caretaker's cottage at Blackthorn and listened as Aurelia called the nursing home to check on her mother. She didn't give any details to the nurses. Aurelia only said that she was unavoidably detained. When she put the telephone down, there were tears in her eyes.

"I'm sorry," Marcus said, going to her. His arms encircled her and he held her tight. He could feel her heart pounding. One of the hardest things about what was happening was her lack of ability to make sure her mother was getting everything she needed.

"I need to go home," she said, the hopeless tone of her voice telling Marcus that she knew it was impossible.

"It won't be long. We can expect a prompt trial date. I don't believe we have any hope the grand jury will throw this out."

"How could this have happened?" she asked.

"I have a better question," Marcus said. "Who would have wanted to frame you for murder?"

Aurelia shook her head. "I can't imagine. I've never done anything to anyone here in Natchez. I've only come to claim what belongs to my mother. Why is someone setting me up for a murder?"

"It isn't personal. Someone wants something you have."

"Blackthorn," she said softly.

Marcus saw that she finally realized exactly what had happened to her. She'd been framed for a murder simply to get her out of the way.

"You don't suppose someone killed Lottie *just* to pin the murder on me, do you?" Aurelia asked.

"If I had the answer to that question, it would make it a lot easier to try and figure out who's behind this."

"Because someone who would do that is totally ruthless," Aurelia said.

Marcus nodded. "You're getting the hang of this." He gave her a quick hug. "We have a limited amount of time, and I think we need to get busy on this right away. I'm going to get Lottie's telephone records. If someone called her and lured her out to Blackthorn, I want to know who that someone is.''

''Joey said she was hunting for the treasure.''

Marcus's eyebrows lifted. ''Joey said that? When?''

''He came by the jail this morning, before the bond hearing. He said Lottie was snooping around Blackthorn looking for the treasure but that Andre didn't want her to have it.''

Marcus turned away, but not before she saw the furrow on his forehead.

''What?'' she asked.

''Did Joey say he *saw* Andre?''

''Andre isn't...real.'' Aurelia's sentence tapered off at the end. ''He's a ghost.''

''You haven't seen him?'' Marcus asked.

''Well,'' Aurelia hedged. ''If I say yes, does that mean we can have an insanity plea in the trial?''

''Have you seen Andre?'' Marcus repeated.

''The first night I was at Blackthorn, I saw something. But the horse and rider went over the cliff at the Mississippi,'' Aurelia said. ''It had to be my imagination.''

''Did Joey say he saw Andre?'' He knew he'd made his point.

''No, he didn't say that. He said Andre didn't like people snooping around. It sounded like he'd sort of blended Lottie's death into the local folklore.'' She hesitated. "You don't think Joey was here, at Black-thorn, the night Lottie was killed, do you?" She couldn't keep the note of excitement out of her voice.

"Joey loves Blackthorn. He comes out here fre-quently, because this is where his best memories are. He's been warned against trespassing out here, but he does it anyway."

"Is what Joey says reliable?" Aurelia asked.

"He wouldn't know how to lie."

"But he believes in Andre. He loves Diable. That doesn't sound like he's exactly living in the real world," Aurelia pointed out.

Marcus strode to the window and looked out. "Damn it all," he whispered.

"What is it?" Aurelia asked, going to him.

He felt her hand on his back, but it gave no com-fort. "We need to talk to Joey."

"If you think it will do any good," Aurelia said.

"Someone's driving up," Marcus said, nodding to the driveway. "It's Yvonne Harris."

He left the window and went to the door, opening it wide before Yvonne could knock. The harried look on the Realtor's face concerned him. "Yvonne," he said, "is something wrong?"

"It's Joey," Yvonne said quickly. "He's missing. I was hoping he'd come up here."

"What do you mean missing?" Marcus knew that Joey often rambled over the town and surrounding area. Everyone around Natchez knew Joey and no one cared that he roamed the fields and orchards.

"He was supposed to clean Mrs. Beckwith's garage today. He never showed up and she called home, worried about him."

Marcus felt a twinge of worry. That wasn't like Joey. He was the most reliable citizen in town. "He was at the jail this morning. He went to see Aurelia."

"What did he say?" Yvonne asked Aurelia. "Did he say anything about going somewhere else?"

"No," Aurelia said, thinking back through the conversation she'd had with Joey. "He didn't say anything at all about what he planned to do. Except that he did ask if he could come out here and visit when I got home."

"He was so upset about Lottie's murder," Yvonne said, wringing her hands. "He likes you, Aurelia, and he kept saying that you didn't do anything wrong."

"That's what he kept saying at the jail."

"I know he was worried about what was going to happen to you, and that probably just made him forget that he'd promised to clean that garage. Mrs. Beckwith is upset, but I'm sure she'll calm down. Right now I'm more worried about Joey than Mrs. Beckwith."

"I'll keep my eye out for him," Marcus promised. "If he comes here, Aurelia will give you a call."

"Thanks. I'm going to check a few more places, then I have to get back to work. I'm so far behind." She looked at Aurelia. "I guess the auction is off."

"For the time being," Marcus answered smoothly. "Since the disposition of Blackthorn seems to be what the sheriff considers the root of the motive for Aurelia to kill Lottie, I think it would be best if we put all plans to sell the estate on hold.''

''Good idea,'' Yvonne agreed, pulling at one of her expensive earrings. ''I'll be in touch.'' She hurried back to her car, driving away as if the demons of hell were on her tail.

AURELIA PACED the confines of the small cottage yet again, wondering what, if anything, Marcus had discovered. He'd asked her to remain at the cottage. The afternoon had passed slowly, each minute seeming to drag on for an eternity.

The telephone rang and she rushed to answer it.

''Aurelia,'' Ella said, ''how are you holding up?''

''I'm fine,'' Aurelia said, making her voice strong. Ella had put up a considerable bond, and Aurelia didn't want to make her think she'd put her money on a weak sister. ''I can't thank you enough for making my bond. It was an incredible thing to do.''

''Posh!'' Ella said. ''Come by the café and get something to eat.''

Aurelia's stomach growled as if it had been cued. The entire day had passed and she hadn't eaten anything. Until this moment, she hadn't been aware she was hungry.

''Marcus asked me to stay here,'' she said, a little chagrined at how timid she sounded.

''Well, you can trot back up to the cottage once you eat something. I insist. The whole town is buzzing about you and the worst thing you can do is act like you're hiding and guilty.''

Aurelia realized the wisdom of Ella's words, but she was hesitant to leave.

''Pin a note to the door. Tell Marcus you're with me. He'll find you, honey. A man who can't track down his woman is a mighty poor specimen of the gender. Trust me, a little tracking makes a man appreciate the prize.''

Aurelia found she was smiling. It seemed like years had passed since she'd smiled. She wanted to be with Ella. She needed the comfort that Ella dispensed as liberally as she did her home cooking.

''I'm on my way.'' She put down the phone, picked up her purse and jacket and headed out the door.

Natchez was in the midst of rush hour as she drove through the old streets toward the café. She passed the television shop where Marcus worked but she didn't see his truck there. He'd told her that his partner had encouraged him to go back into the law. It seemed several people in Natchez had a loving interest in Marcus's career.

She parked in a far corner of the lot at the café and hurried inside. The afternoon was waning and there was a cutting wind off the river.

Stepping into the café was like being enfolded in safety. The scent of fresh-baked apple pie mingled with coffee and the lemony scent of pound cake. Aurelia's mouth watered.

"Come right on in here," Ella called to her when Aurelia stopped inside the door.

Aurelia felt the gaze of all the patrons turn to her. Whereas before she'd been the stranger in Natchez, now she felt a different kind of interest in the stares.

"That's her," a woman several tables away whispered. "She's the one who killed Lottie Levert."

Aurelia started to deny such an outrageous charge, but she felt Ella's firm hand on her elbow, guiding her past the staring patrons.

"You just sit down right here and start with a cup of good, fresh coffee," Ella said, pouring the coffee into a thick mug as she talked. "Marlis has made the best country-fried steak you've ever wrapped your lips around. She's fixing you a plate with some home-made mashed potatoes, gravy and some tomatoes and okra. Probably not as good as what grows around here in season, but it's the best we could do on a winter day.

"It sounds wonderful," Aurelia said, distressed to find that she was almost whispering. She hated the idea that people were staring at her, talking about her, spreading gossip.

There was an outburst of giggles from the table with the woman who'd called Aurelia a killer. Ella patted Aurelia's arm. "I've been itching to do this for forty years, and now I have the perfect reason."

Aurelia started to protest, but she wasn't fast enough. Ella was across the restaurant, her finger in the talkative woman's face.

"Ethel Malone, you should be ashamed. All you do is say ugly things about people."

"She's charged with Lottie's murder," Ethel said in a voice that spoke of her superiority. "It's just like you, Ella, to take up with someone who is capable of killing."

"What's wrong, Ethel? Are you jealous that someone beat you to the punch? I've heard you many a day sit right in that chair and talk about how much you'd like to wring Lottie's neck. In fact, I think I'll call the sheriff right now and tell him all about it."

"Don't be a fool," Ethel said. "No one would believe such a thing."

"Because you're Ethel Malone," Ella said. "Because you live here. The only reason Aurelia is even suspected is because she's an outsider."

"She's suspected because she threatened Lottie."

"She didn't. And if threats were the basis for murder charges, you'd be in jail the rest of your life."

"Well, I never!" Ethel stood up, her friends scrambling to follow suit. "I won't be back here, Ella. Nor will any of my friends."

Aurelia didn't miss the distressed look that passed over the faces of the other two women with Ethel Malone.

"And my café will be a nicer place if you don't come back," Ella said. "I don't need your kind of trash-talking riffraff as a customer."

Ethel's face grew an ugly, splotched pink. "You'll regret this, Ella. I'll see to it."

"Another threat," Ella said, totally unperturbed. "I'll mention that to the sheriff when he arrives. You'd better pray nothing bad happens to me."

Ethel slammed a twenty-dollar bill down on the table and stormed out of the café. In the corner two middle-aged men applauded.

"She's had that coming all of her life," one of the men said.

"Way to go, Ella," the other added.

As soon as the bell on the door stopped jangling, Ella returned to the counter where Aurelia sat.

"I'm so sorry," Aurelia said. "I shouldn't have come in here."

"Nonsense. As I told you, I've been itching to tell that old bat off for years. I just never did it because, well, because I didn't get mad enough to do it. Today, I got mad." She walked around the counter and picked up a plate steaming with hot mashed potatoes and gravy. Putting it down in front of Aurelia, she turned to get a glass of iced tea.

"So where is Marcus?"

"I don't know," Aurelia said, realizing that when he was absent she felt as if her whole world had stopped.

"Digging up evidence, I'd say."

"Yes, I'm sure. I wish he'd let me go with him."

Ella shook her head. "Sometimes it's best to let him do it. Folks around here know him. They might talk to him easier if he's alone."

"Right. I'm the stranger. The outsider."

Ella gave her a quick hug. "That's right, and some folks are terrified of something new. Now me, I think it's time we got some new blood in this old town. Now you eat before you dry up and blow away."

Aurelia lifted a forkful of mashed potatoes and gravy to her mouth. It was so good she sighed. "I've never eaten food like this."

"I can tell," Ella said, laughing. "You've got the figure of a teenager."

"I could give up a few dress sizes to eat like this," Aurelia said, taking a bite of the steak. She rolled her eyes. "I think I'm in heaven."

"I got in a flat of strawberries this morning. The best ones come from Louisiana, but they aren't ripe until the spring. These we got today are from California. Marlis and I picked the best ones and we made a pie." Her eyebrows lifted. "Nothing like a fresh strawberry pie to chase away the blues."

Aurelia looked at her plate. "I don't know if I have room, but I'm willing to try."

"That's the spirit." Ella turned to the kitchen. "One slice of strawberry, Marlis."

The bell over the door jangled and Ella was still laughing when she turned to see who was coming in. Her laughter died abruptly, causing Aurelia to spin around on her stool. Dru Colson stood in the doorway, his hat in his hands and a worried expression on his face.

"There's been an accident," he said slowly. "Marcus has been injured. He's at the hospital."

Chapter Fourteen

Aurelia wasn't even aware that Ella had gotten into the passenger seat of her car as she pulled out of the parking lot and raced to the hospital.

"Slow down, honey," Ella said, putting a hand on Aurelia's arm.

Aurelia glanced down at the speedometer and realized she was doing seventy-five in a fifty-mile zone. She slowed, but her hands gripped tighter on the wheel.

"The sheriff didn't say how bad Marcus was hurt. What does that mean?" Aurelia asked.

"With Dru, it doesn't mean one thing or another. If Marcus was critical, I promise you, Dru would have taken you in the cruiser."

"Are you sure?" Aurelia asked.

"I'm positive," Ella said firmly. "Get a grip on your imagination. See Marcus in your mind—see him sitting up in bed, smiling when you enter the room."

"Do you see that?" Aurelia asked hopefully.

"I can't lie, honey. I don't see that, but I don't see anything bad, either. You can't rely on my sight, though, you have to develop your own."

"All I want right now is for Marcus to be okay." She pulled the car into a parking place near the emergency room door.

"Go on, honey," Ella said. "I'll be right behind you."

Aurelia took off at a run, stopping at the desk where she breathlessly asked about Marcus. The nurse directed her to a seat in the waiting room, saying that Marcus was being held in an examining room for observation.

Instead of sitting, Aurelia ignored the nurse and hurried to the cluster of examining rooms. She found Marcus on the first try. He was sitting on the side of a table, a worried look on his face. A long gash on his forehead had been stitched together.

"Aurelia," he said, rubbing a hand over his forehead. "Don't look so worried."

"Are you okay?" she asked, not caring that her voice trembled and tears had begun to run down her cheeks.

"I'm okay, but my truck may not survive." He tried for a smile. When Aurelia didn't respond, he held out his arms.

Aurelia ran across the room to him, burying her face in his chest. "I was so frightened," she said, holding him tight.

"I'm fine," he reassured her. "But I have to say,

I'd get hurt every day if I thought I could get this kind of reaction from you.''

"Oh, Marcus.'' She eased back from him, brushing the tears from her cheeks. "What happened?''

"It's just a little bump on the head,'' Marcus said. "The steering on the truck went out and I hit a tree on Willow Street.''

Aurelia let her gaze move over his body. The only injury seemed to be his head. There was blood on his shirt, but it looked as if it had come from the cut.

"Are you sure you're okay?''

"I'm positive. In fact, I'm waiting for the doctor to release me. They just wanted me to stay here for a little while to be sure. How'd you find out I was hurt?''

"Dru came and told me.'' Aurelia suddenly remembered that Ella had come with her to the hospital. "Ella's in the waiting room. I should go tell her you're okay.''

"Now that I have you to drive me home, I think they'll let me go, too.'' Marcus eased to his feet as he was talking. He was a little wobbly, but after a few steps he regained his balance.

The door to the room swung open and a young doctor gave Marcus an assessing glance. "Looks like you're ready to go,'' he said.

"Is he okay?'' Aurelia asked.

"What, you don't believe me when I tell you I'm okay?'' Marcus teased her.

"I'd prefer to hear it from a medical authority," Aurelia replied.

"He's good to go," the doctor said to Aurelia. "Just keep an eye on him. He took a severe bump on the head, but he seems fine." He turned to Marcus. "If you feel any disorientation, any stabbing pains, you need to come back here immediately."

"I will," Marcus said.

"Good luck." The doctor moved on to the next room where another patient waited.

Aurelia held Marcus's arm as they walked out into the waiting room. Ella's face lit up when she saw them. She hurried toward them, her pale-blue eyes roving over Marcus as she summed up his wounds.

"Lucky it was your head that hit whatever it hit," she said quickly. "That's the hardest part of him," she whispered sotto voce to Aurelia.

"Make fun all you want," Marcus said. "Here I am, gravely injured, and all you want to do is pick on me."

"Poor, poor man," Ella consoled him with a glint of mischief in her eyes. "How about we take you home, tuck you into bed, and then I'll bring you a home-cooked meal?"

"Food," Marcus said, suddenly leaning more heavily on Aurelia. "I'm weak because I haven't eaten." He bent so that he could whisper in Aurelia's ear. "I may need physical therapy."

Ella laughed. "I can see you're going to milk this situation for all it's worth."

"I fully intend to," Marcus agreed.

Aurelia was so relieved to see that Marcus was okay that she would have agreed to almost anything he asked. Together the three of them walked to the car. Marcus agreeably got into the passenger seat.

"What happened to your truck?" Ella asked from the back seat as they drove away from the hospital.

"That's a good question." Marcus's joking nature was gone. "I was driving down Willow Street. A cat darted in front of the truck and I swerved to miss it. I did miss the cat, but the truck became completely unresponsive. I managed to slow down a little before I hit an oak tree. A woman saw the accident and called 911 on her cell phone. The ambulance and Dru arrived about the same time."

"The steering went out?" Aurelia asked, her sense of relief beginning to give way to foreboding. "Just like that? Where had you been?"

Marcus gave her a look of approval. "You're thinking exactly what I'm thinking. Someone may have tampered with the truck. I was at the church. I went to look around for Joey. He has a small apartment in the back."

"And it was fine when you stopped there?" Aurelia pressed.

"Perfect. It was handling like a dream. I just had it checked out two weeks ago."

"How long were you at the church?" Ella asked.

"About twenty minutes."

"And you were parked on the street right in front of the church?" Aurelia asked.

"No, I'd pulled around behind the meeting chapel."

Aurelia frowned. "So no one could see the truck," she guessed.

"Exactly. I'm concerned about Joey, and I didn't want everyone in town to know I was looking for him."

The sense of dread made Aurelia feel as if a heavy rock was on her chest. "You think someone did something to Joey because he's my friend?"

Aurelia felt Ella's hand rub her shoulder, but it was Marcus who answered. "No, not because he's your friend, but because he may have seen something he shouldn't have seen."

Aurelia pulled the car in front of the café and stopped. She turned to face Marcus. "Did someone deliberately disable your truck?"

"Maybe. Dru will know soon enough. If the power steering lines were cut, Dru will be able to tell."

"I'm worried about the two of you," Ella said. "Someone murdered Lottie Levert. If you become a threat to them, they might hurt either or both of you."

"We'll be okay," Marcus said. "In order to prove Aurelia innocent, we're going to have to find the real killer. I never thought it would be easy."

"We have to find Joey first," Aurelia said. She was more worried about the young man than herself. Joey was so gentle and innocent. Even if he had seen something the night of Lottie's murder, he wouldn't know how important it could be.

"You two be careful," Ella said. "I'll keep my ears open in the café. If I can do anything to help, just let me know." She got out of the car, leaned in the passenger window and gave Marcus a kiss on the cheek. "Call me," she said, waving to Aurelia before she went back into the café.

MARCUS ALLOWED Aurelia to drive him to his house. While she ran a hot bath for him, he took the portable phone to the front porch and called the sheriff's office.

"When was the last time you had your car checked?" Dru asked him, his voice revealing nothing.

"Two weeks ago. Tony Nuccio went over it."

"He's a good mechanic," Dru said.

"Yes, he is," Marcus agreed, waiting for Dru to say more.

"The power steering lines were cut," Dru finally said. "I found a puddle of steering fluid where you'd parked behind the church chapel."

"Damn," Marcus was still finding it hard to believe that someone had deliberately tried to kill him.

"You didn't see anyone?"

"No," Marcus said.

"What were you doing there?" Dru asked.

Marcus realized that no one had told the sheriff that Joey Reynolds was missing. "Yvonne Harris came by the caretaker's cottage before noon. She said Joey had failed to show up for some job. She was a little worried about Joey, so I decided to stop by his place and see if I could find him.''

There was a long pause before Dru came back on the line. ''It's nearly five now. Joey's been missing all day? Who saw him last?''

''He was at the jail about nine this morning, visiting Aurelia. That was the last anyone's seen of him.''

''I'll see if I can find him,'' Dru said. ''I want you and Aurelia to get in one place and stay there. Okay?''

''We'll be fine,'' Marcus said.

''I know you will be, if you do what I'm asking.''

Marcus took a deep breath. ''I can't promise you anything, Dru. Aurelia's charged with a murder she didn't commit. We can't sit around and hope someone else confesses.''

''Marcus, it looks like someone tried to kill you. I'd take that a little more seriously if I were you.''

''I'll be careful,'' Marcus said. ''You have my word on that.''

''Where's Aurelia?''

''She's here, at my house.''

''Keep her there. I don't like the idea of her being up at Blackthorn alone.''

''I'll do my best,'' Marcus said.

As he was hanging up the phone, he realized Aurelia was standing in the doorway.

"Your hot bath is ready, and I put on a pot of coffee. I'd forgotten how nice it is to have an automatic coffeemaker."

Marcus went to her, his arms circling her and holding her against him. "Dru is concerned for you," he said. "He wants you to stay here."

"As long as you're here," she said.

He rubbed his hands along her back. "We just want to keep you safe, Aurelia," he said.

"I'm fine right here with you." She stood on tiptoe and kissed his cheek. "But you need a hot bath. Your muscles are going to be sore. And I know all about sore muscles," she said, smiling. "I almost couldn't walk this morning when I got up. I think I need more hours in the saddle."

"We'll make sure that happens." He kissed her, long and slow, enjoying every moment.

"I could stand a little more of that," she said, breathless, when he finally released her. "After your bath." She tugged his hands, pulling him toward the bathroom.

"While you're bathing, I'll run to Ella's and pick up something for you to eat. Save her a trip. I know she's trying to close up the café."

AURELIA PULLED the blanket over Marcus's chest and took a seat in the chair beside the sofa where he slept. He'd eaten and fallen sound asleep. His blond hair looked gilded in the light from the lamp. In fact, Marcus looked positively angelic, but it was only because he was asleep. She smiled at the thought and realized how much he'd come to mean to her.

She was in love with him. He was kind and gentle, reliable and responsible, giving and generous. He was all the things she'd never expected to find in a man. Marcus was one in a million.

And he loved her back. That was the most amazing thing. As a child, she'd missed having a father. Her mother had worked hard and made a superhuman effort to provide Aurelia with all the things other children had. When she became a teenager and her mother had told her how her father had abandoned them both, it had broken Aurelia's heart—and made her fear that all men were unreliable.

Marcus had taught her that wasn't true. He was right here at her side during the worst time of her life. Risking everything, he'd promised to help her. How would she ever leave him, once Blackthorn was sold?

He shifted on the sofa and Aurelia saw his blue eyes open. She smiled when he saw her and surprise registered on his face.

"Hey, when I woke up and saw you, I thought maybe I was in heaven," he said, smiling as he stretched.

"How are you?"

"Sore, but other than that, just fine."

"Are you sure?" Aurelia asked, her hand lightly tracing the skin beside his wound.

"I'm positive." He pushed himself up to a sitting position. "I need to check on a few things."

Aurelia rose to her feet. "It's nearly seven o'clock."

"It's okay. I want to talk to Randall. It'll probably be better if I talk to him after work."

"I'll drive you. You shouldn't be driving."

He stood, putting both arms around her. "I'm fine. I promise. It would be better if I talked to him alone. I wouldn't leave you but I'm hoping I can make him understand the consequences of perjury. He's lying when he says you threatened him. If I can convince him to tell the truth, maybe we can start searching for the real killer."

"Take my rental car," she said, pulling the keys from her pocket.

"Will you be okay here?" he lifted her chin so that she looked directly into his eyes. "No one except Dru knows you're here and I'll be back soon."

"I'll be fine."

"And I'll be back as quick as I can."

AURELIA WASHED the few dishes they'd dirtied, picked up the television remote and scanned the channels, and finally picked up a magazine on gardening.

She was deep in an article on planting bulbs when the telephone rang. She picked it up instinctively.

"Aurelia?" The voice was muffled, but she could tell it belonged to a man.

"Yes, who is this?" she asked.

"You should have sold Blackthorn when you had

the chance. Now you'll never sell the estate. Andre doesn't want you to sell it.''

''Who is this?'' Her heart had begun to pound furiously. Who knew she was at Marcus's house? Someone must have been following her, watching her. She looked around at all the windows in the room. Was someone watching her even as she talked on the phone?

''It doesn't matter who I am. You're looking for that man who lives at the church, aren't you?''

''Where's Joey?'' The metallic taste of fear made her gasp. Joey was in trouble. She knew it.

''He's at Blackthorn. And he's in danger.''

The phone went dead.

Chapter Fifteen

Marcus slipped behind a potted palm at the edge of the showroom floor. He'd made it inside the door just in time. The lot closed at seven, and Randall had been ready to lock up for the night when a young couple arrived to look at a used SUV. That had given Marcus the diversion he needed to get inside without Randall seeing him. But the car salesman was ready to leave.

Marcus heard the impatience in Randall's voice. He was barely civil as he answered the questions the young couple kept asking about the vehicle.

"Will the warranty cover the transmission?" the woman asked. Randall was so aggravated that it was the perfect moment for Marcus to ease into Randall's private office. The light was on, and Marcus surveyed the room, taking in the expensive furniture. The neat desk.

It gave Marcus some pleasure to know that if the car salesman knew he was waiting on him, Randall wouldn't be in any hurry to finish up with his customers.

Taking a seat in Randall's chair, Marcus listened to the conversation drifting to him from the showroom floor. The wife was saying they'd be back in the morning. Marcus sat up taller in the chair. He was facing the door when Randall walked in.

"What are you doing here?" Randall asked angrily. He waved one hand at Marcus. "Get out of my chair."

Marcus stood up, walked past Randall and closed the office door with a none too gentle slam. "You lied to Dru." He turned blazing blue eyes on Randall.

"Who do you think you are, coming in here and accusing me of lying? You'd stoop to anything to protect that woman." Randall reached behind him and opened the door. "Get out of here before I call the law on you."

"I know Aurelia, and I know she didn't threaten you or your mother. If you want to find the real killer, you should tell the truth."

"I'm telling the truth," Randall said, a grim smile on his face. "If you could prove otherwise, you wouldn't be here now. What are you trying to do, intimidate me? You don't have a lot of ammunition, Marcus. Get out of here before you make matters worse for your girlfriend."

"Randall, Aurelia didn't kill Lottie. I don't know why you want to pretend that she did. I came here to point out to you that while Aurelia is being prosecuted, the real murderer is free."

Randall shook his head slowly. "If that's the best

defense you can come up with, I see another client of yours is destined for prison.''

Marcus felt a rush of hot anger, but he controlled it. Randall was a liar who only knew how to throw cheap shots. ''Just keep this in mind, Randall. If Lottie was killed because of Blackthorn, then you may be next in line for extermination.''

''Are you threatening me?'' Randall asked with an edge of nervousness.

''Don't be a fool. I have no desire to hurt you and neither does Aurelia. But someone else may. I'd watch my back if I were you. Once you give your lying testimony against Aurelia, your usefulness will be done.'' Marcus opened the door and walked out.

''I'm filing an injunction to stop the sale of Blackthorn,'' Randall said to Marcus's back.

Marcus turned around. ''I was a little surprised to see that you were open today, Randall. Will you close for your mother's funeral service?'' He saw with some satisfaction that he'd hit a nerve. Without waiting for an answer, he walked out into the night.

The exchange hadn't gone well, but it had been exactly what he expected. Randall had lied when he'd told Dru that Aurelia had threatened him at the dance. Getting him to tell the truth was not going to be easy.

Marcus got into Aurelia's car. He was eager to get home to her. The wreck had taken the starch out of his sails, but he was beginning to feel much better. He drove home with anticipation at the thought of Aurelia in his bed.

Pulling into the drive, he had the strangest sense that his house was empty. That was impossible, though. Aurelia was there. She didn't have a car.

He hurried inside, calling her name as he went. When there was no answer, he felt a knot of dread in his chest.

"Aurelia?" he called.

There was only emptiness.

"Aurelia?" he hurried through the rooms of the house, even checking the closets. There was no sign of Aurelia. The house was wide-open. Had someone abducted her? Panic began to block out rational thought, and he fought it. He had to call Dru. Someone had taken Aurelia. He went to the phone and started to dial when he noticed the note written on a pad beside the phone.

"I've gone to Blackthorn. Joey is in trouble."

AURELIA PAID the taxi driver and watched the taillights disappear with a sense of foreboding. The driver had been reluctant to leave her at Blackthorn alone, especially halfway up the drive. Perhaps she should have heeded his concerns.

She took a deep breath and walked quietly up the remaining portion of the drive until she could see the cabin. There was no one about, but she had to go inside. She had to see if Joey was there, injured—or worse. It was dark, and she realized her hand was trembling as she inserted the key. Pushing the door open, she held her breath. She halfway expected someone to jump out of the darkness and grab her. But the door swung open on a groaning hinge. Black emptiness yawned at her.

Stepping into the darkness, she felt for the light and flipped it on. Nothing happened. She tried the switch again, flipping it up and down. Damn! The power lines were down. First the phone, now the power. Stumbling forward she went to the telephone. The smartest thing to do would be to call another cab, go back to Marcus's house and wait for him. Together they could return to Blackthorn and search for Joey. The telephone call had panicked her and she'd rushed out without any idea what she should do. Her impulse had simply been to get to Joey. Now she was beginning to realize that she'd acted without thought.

She inched forward until she found the telephone and brought the receiver to her ear only to discover that the phone was dead. Again.

Almost afraid to breathe, she replaced the receiver. The only way back to town was to walk. Or ride Mariah—if she could find her way back to the stables again. She vetoed that idea, realizing she wasn't a good enough rider to attempt to take the horse into town.

One thing was certain, though: she had no intention of staying at Blackthorn without a phone or electricity.

With a sense of relief, she remembered the flashlight beneath the kitchen sink. That, at least, would allow her to see where she was going. She felt her way around the unfamiliar cabin until she got to the sink. She knocked over several things before her fingers found the cylindrical shape of the flashlight. Clicking it on, she let out a sigh of relief as the strong beam of light illuminated the cabin.

She checked her watch. It was a little after seven. Marcus would be home before long. He'd find her note and come after her. The smartest thing she could do would be to wait for him to arrive. She bit her lip as she thought about how angry he'd be. She had gone off half-cocked when she rushed out of the house, hoping to find Joey at Blackthorn. If she'd thought things through, she would have waited for Marcus.

But the caller had sounded so…scary. There had been an urgency in his voice. Thinking about it, Aurelia knew when she rushed to Blackthorn that she was possibly walking into a trap. But what trap? No one was anywhere around.

Clicking off the light, she made her way outside the cottage and started down the path to the old burial mound. If she'd been tricked into coming to Blackthorn, the worst place she could stay would be the cottage. If she could scale the mound, she'd be able to watch the path and see if anyone was sneaking around. She glanced up at the sky and thanked the fates that it wasn't overcast. A clear, three-quarter moon gave some light.

She made her way around the old pillars, stopping to listen when she thought she heard someone slipping through the fallen leaves. Straining to see into the dark forest, she finally convinced herself that the noise was made by birds or other small forest creatures scuttling around.

Taking a breath, she leaned against one of the pillars. Blackthorn must have been grand at one time, sitting on land high above the river. She could easily imagine the old antebellum house. What a shame that Andre Agee had been murdered by a mob and that his house had been destroyed.

The pillar was rough under her hand. Somehow, though it gave her comfort to touch it. Like the old pillar, Rachel, the wife of Andre and her ancestor, had survived a lot. Aurelia knew she would get through this false accusation, too.

She started toward the old mound. It was going to be tricky climbing it at night, but she could do it. It was the safest place she could be at Blackthorn. From the top of the mound, she'd be able to see Marcus's headlights coming down the drive, and she had no doubt that once he found her note he would come to Blackthorn to help her.

She started up the mound. The trees around the base were thick and threw dense shadows on the incline as she began to scale it. Aurelia didn't see the hole. Her right leg went in so suddenly that she was pitched headfirst into the blackness. She struck the ground so hard that it knocked the breath out of her, and for a moment she was afraid that she'd broken something. When at last she managed to drag some air back into her lungs, she assessed the damage and realized that she wasn't seriously hurt. She'd have a few good bruises, but luckily nothing was broken.

She lay at the bottom of the hole, trying to think through what had happened. The hole hadn't been there the last time she'd climbed the mound. This was more than a hole. It was a pit. It was at least six feet deep and large enough…for a coffin. The thought sent goose bumps dancing over her skin. It was, in fact, so deep that she couldn't see over the top. But the dirt was soft, and she was able to dig her fingers and toes into the side of the pit and begin to climb out.

As her arms reached out of the pit and grabbed grass, she felt the soft dirt crumbling beneath her feet. She gave a mighty heave, trying to throw herself out of the pit. She'd managed to get her upper body out and onto the grassy bank when she saw something that made her stop her frantic struggles—a pair of men's shoes only inches from her face.

Craning her neck up, she saw jean-clad legs that led to a broad leather belt. Before she could look further, a bright light cut into her vision.

"Hey!" she said.

There was no sound. Aurelia was totally unprepared for the foot against her forehead as she was pushed back into the pit. The last thing she felt was her back striking the dirt with tremendous force. Her head landed with a thump and the darkness was complete.

MARCUS OVERCOMPENSATED for the sharp curve in the drive as he rushed toward Blackthorn. He was used to his old truck; the more compact car Aurelia had rented was quicker. He spun the wheel, stepped on the gas and scattered gravel as he sped toward the caretaker's cottage.

The cottage was totally dark, and when he tried the door, it opened on a squeaky hinge. He knew Aurelia wasn't there. Something had happened to her. He could feel it. He had to find her, and he had to protect her.

He left the cottage and got back in the car. Turning around, he headed toward the road. He drove for half a mile along the highway before he made a sharp left turn into a rutted lane that disappeared into the blackness of the trees. When he'd driven half a mile down the narrow lane at breakneck speed, he got out of the car and began to run. Five minutes later he burst into a clearing that contained a solidly built barn. He was greeted by a loud whinny. "Easy, Diable," he whispered as he changed from his jeans to black pants and a white shirt. Minutes later he had the huge black Andalusian saddled. He strapped a sword to his waist, flung a cape over his shoulder, and mounted the prancing black horse.

Aurelia Agee was somewhere on the premises of Blackthorn. He was certain of that. And someone had deliberately lured her to the old estate. While her abductor held the high card, Marcus had the joker. No one would be expecting Andre Agee to ride to the rescue. He would have the element of surprise, and hopefully, of fear. It was the only thing he had going in his favor.

AURELIA AWOKE with a thudding pain in her head. She'd slammed hard into the dirt. And she had no idea how long she'd been unconscious. Down in the hole, it was too dark to see her watch and she'd dropped the flashlight somewhere.

Moving slowly, she got to her feet. She had to get out of the pit, but she was afraid to try. What if the person who'd kicked her was still standing there, waiting for her to make another attempt to climb out?

But what was her alternative? She couldn't stay in the hole. Her assailant might try to bury her alive! And Marcus would be worried sick. She had no doubt that he'd made it back to his house and found the note. In all probability he was somewhere on Blackthorn searching for her.

Unless the whole episode had been set up to lure Marcus to Blackthorn!

Her heart began to race and she started digging her hands into the sides of the hole. Marcus could be in jeopardy because of her. She had to get out of the hole and find him—before someone else did.

She was halfway up the side of the pit when she heard the frantic crying of the baby. She paused and listened. It was impossible to tell where the crying was coming from, but it sounded as if it were somewhere very near the burial mound.

The muscles of her legs were quivering from the strain of the climb. Her arms felt leaden, but she pushed herself. At last she got her upper torso out of the hole. Digging her fingers into the thick grass, she pulled her hips and legs free. Exhausted, she wanted only to lie in the grass and rest. But that was a luxury she couldn't afford. She had to find Marcus.

She got to her feet and paused to listen to the sound of the baby crying. The poor infant sounded so pitiful and scared. Logically, though, she knew that if an infant had been abandoned at Blackthorn for as long as she'd been hearing the baby cry, the child would be dead. No infant could survive days and nights without food or water in such cold weather.

The next question that popped into her mind made her skin prickle with goose bumps once again. So what kind of baby would be crying for nights on end?

Not a living baby.

Andre Agee wasn't the only ghost haunting Blackthorn.

As if her words brought the specter to life, she heard the sound of hoofbeats. Running to the edge of the mound, she saw the ghostly white of the driveway in the moonlight.

The dark shadow of horse and rider burst from the trees. The huge horse galloped down the drive, sparks flying where his iron hooves struck the pale gravel.

Aurelia staggered backward. She caught her balance, her gaze riveted to the terrifying figure of the horse and rider racing through the night.

Andre Agee had returned to Blackthorn. Had he come as friend or foe? She didn't know.

MARCUS LET DIABLE have his head. The powerful horse, eager for a run, galloped through the night. Marcus's right hand touched the grip of his sword. He'd never drawn a weapon with the intention of using it. But tonight was different. He would do whatever he had to do to protect Aurelia.

If only he could find her.

His anxiety was telegraphed to the horse, and Diable answered by lengthening his stride. Marcus saw the pillars of the old estate in front of him. He was acting on instinct. If Aurelia had left the cottage, he felt she must have come in the direction of the pillars.

A dark spot in the drive caught his attention. He pulled Diable up and stared down at the black glove that had fallen in the lane. As he stopped, he heard the mournful sound of a baby's hopeless cry. The glove was Aurelia's. He recognized it. Had she tossed it down deliberately or had it slipped from her pocket?

He had no way of knowing the answer to that, but he did know that he was headed in the right direction. Aurelia had traveled this way. Nudging the horse with his calves, he urged Diable forward, trying to judge the direction from which the baby's cry came.

Someone else was in the woods of Blackthorn. Someone, or something.

That was no live baby crying. But the man who'd

worked so hard to keep the legend of Blackthorn alive paused in the night and listened to what sounded like the spirit of a long-departed infant drift through the night.

Chapter Sixteen

Aurelia was transfixed by the sight of the horse and rider. They were positively ghostly—or demonic—if one believed in such things. They thundered through the night, the horse stretching long and covering the ground in effortless strides.

Only the sparks flying from the horse's shoes indicated that the huge beast actually touched the ground. That and the pounding of the soil.

Aurelia saw the rider pull the horse up as he jumped to the ground to pick something up. Her glove! She realized what it was and her heart felt as if it might burst. Andre Agee knew she was on the grounds of Blackthorn. And he scanned the area, looking for her.

Mist blew from the horse's nostrils, giving it the look of something from hell. Aurelia felt her lungs stop and her scalp began to prickle with a sensation that signaled trouble.

She couldn't afford to faint. Drawing air deep into

her lungs, she focused on the man and the horse. Even standing still, they conveyed the essence of power and action.

The mournful wail of the baby came again, and she watched as Andre began to track the sound, too. He froze for a moment, and in one swift movement, vaulted onto the saddle. The horse barely waited for him to settle his feet in the stirrups before they were off, headed toward the pillars.

Aurelia watched in growing horror as horse and rider passed the thicket of devil's walking sticks and turned toward the burial mound. It was as if the caped and masked rider could sense her presence. Aurelia had never believed in ghosts or bogeymen or monsters, but she knew in her heart that the man on the black horse was something extraordinary. What she didn't know was if he was human. He seemed more wraith than flesh and blood.

The sounds of the crying infant ceased as suddenly as they'd begun. There was only the tattoo of the horse's hooves as it raced through the night.

Even though she was still shaken by her fall into the pit, Aurelia started running. Her legs were rubbery at first, but she gained strength as she ran. When she got to the edge of the mound, she trusted blind faith and skittered down it, almost crashing into the tree line at the base.

She could feel the ground shaking with the coming of the horse. No matter what awaited her in the woods, she was too afraid to confront Andre. She'd believed him a legend—a spooky story created and designed to discourage trespassing. Now, he was more than a legend. She'd seen him, and she knew that she was connected to him in a way that defied logic.

He was coming *for* her.

Rushing into the trees, she found a clump of dense undergrowth and hid behind it as the horse and rider passed by her. Her impulse was to close her eyes, but she couldn't. She watched as the duo sped by not ten yards from where she hid. She could almost feel the heat coming from the horse's body as it raced by. She caught a glimpse of Andre's profile, his face unrecognizable behind a mask. She saw the sword at his thigh and knew exactly how it would look in the glint of moonlight.

And then horse and rider were gone. They'd passed her by and hadn't seen her. Hadn't sensed her hiding place as she feared they might.

Relief was almost tangible as she held on to the trunk of a small tree and took a few deep breaths. Andre and his horse disappeared into the night. They had been swallowed by the dense forest. Even the pounding of the hooves was fading. She pulled herself to her feet, trembling with both fear and relief.

The thought of Joey pierced her relief. She might be safe, but what of Joey? Where was he? And what danger was he in?

She'd come to Blackthorn because she knew Joey

needed her. As much as she wanted to go home, that wasn't an option. She had to find Joey. She had to.

Moving out of her hiding place, she started around the base of the burial mound to find the path that led into the woods. If Joey wasn't in the caretaker's cottage, then he might be hiding somewhere in the woods. She'd have to trust to the hope that if he saw her, he'd call out to her, because she knew that she'd never find him in the dense foliage.

Moving carefully, she made her way down the path. The moon was fairly bright, but its pale light was lost in the dense leaves. She held one hand out in front of her, pushing the small branches out of her way. Every step made her realize how much she wished she'd stayed and waited for Marcus. And where was he? What could be keeping him? She was certain that as soon as he read the note she'd left he would be on his way to Blackthorn. But there had been no sign of him.

Worry for Joey was supplanted by her sudden concern for Marcus. Only tragedy would have kept him from coming to Blackthorn. She hadn't forgotten that someone had already tired to kill him that day.

Perhaps the phone call to his home had been designed to get her out of the way so someone could hurt Marcus. She picked up the pace of her walking, ignoring the sting of an occasional branch as it slapped across her face. She'd decided to circle around the woods and try to get back to the driveway.

Once there she could walk to the highway, and then

she'd flag down a ride. It didn't matter how she did it, but she had to get back to town and to Marcus.

A small tree limb slapped into her cheek and brought tears to her eyes. She stopped long enough to rub the wound, blinking away the sting. She was about to go forward again when she heard the sound of the baby crying once more.

The sound was close. She listened intently, judging the direction to be southwest. Torn between going back to check on Marcus or finding the source of the baby's crying, she hesitated. Then she saw the figure darting among the trees.

She started to call out to the figure, then thought better of it. Instead, she began running after him, aware that she was headed in the direction of the crying baby—and away from the cottage. She was going deeper and deeper into the woods of Blackthorn.

The man was quick. Several times she thought she'd lost him, but he'd reappear, just ahead, darting through the trees. He seemed to be following the cries of the baby. And he was running as if he knew every inch of the ground he covered.

Aurelia was gaining on him slowly. She pushed her body, forcing her legs to churn and her feet to fly over the uneven ground. If she thought about it, she knew she might trip and fall. But she kept her gaze on the fleeing figure and her legs moving her forward.

The man zigged out of the trees and stopped. He turned, listening for the baby.

"Joey!" Aurelia recognized him and felt a rush of relief. Joey wasn't hurt. But he was at Blackthorn.

He turned toward her, his face drawing into a look of concern.

"Miss Aurelia," he said. "Go away from here."

"Joey!" She was panting and exhausted and she allowed her body to stop. "I've been looking for you," she gasped. "We've been worried about you."

"Go away from here!" Joey said, growing agitated. "Now!" He pointed in the direction she'd come. "This place is not good for you."

"Come with me," she said, ready, for the moment, to ignore the ghostly crying of the baby. She wanted out of the woods. Joey was safe, and if she could convince him to leave with her, she'd be perfectly delighted to leave Blackthorn. She'd go straight to Marcus to make sure that he was safe and then they could get the entire sheriff's department or the National Guard to find out why there was the sound of a crying baby in her woods.

"Go," Joey said, rocking with agitation. "Get away. I have to find the baby."

"There is no baby." Aurelia was certain of it. Whatever made the sound, it wasn't a real baby. "Come with me, Joey. We'll get Marcus."

"Can't," Joey said, becoming even more agitated. "Go away, Miss Aurelia. Go now, before—" He stopped as the sound of distant hooves grew in the distance. "Andre is coming!"

He turned and began to run. Aurelia started after

him, but she instantly saw that he was leaving her behind. She called his name, but he never even turned around. He just kept running and she didn't have the stamina to catch him again.

''Joey!''

She watched as he disappeared in the dense trees and she was left all alone in the woods of Blackthorn with the ghostly wail of a baby and the sound of pounding hooves as Andre Agee and Diable returned.

MARCUS LET DIABLE pick his own path through the woods as they doubled back in an attempt to find Aurelia. He'd lost her in the darkness. He'd hoped that she might attempt to find the stables where Mariah and Cogar were kept, but he'd ridden there only to find no trace of her.

Now he'd come back, wondering if she was in pursuit of the crying infant. Someone was deliberately manipulating the sound—much as he'd manipulated the legend of Andre Agee and his black hell-horse. But who? And why would they use a baby? Because Aurelia wouldn't be able to ignore the sound of an injured or frightened child. He knew the answer, and it made him press his legs more firmly against Diable's sides, sending the horse surging forward.

Marcus intended to have all his questions answered to his complete satisfaction—as soon as he found Aurelia. He was worried about her. He had no doubt that someone had tricked her into coming to Blackthorn. And that someone could only have ulterior motives.

He had to figure out what was going on. Someone had tried to kill him. He accepted that. He'd lived his entire life in Natchez and had done nothing to earn anyone's hatred or fear—until he'd befriended Aurelia. But he felt he wasn't the target. Aurelia was.

Someone had framed Aurelia for the murder of Lottie Levert. But why? Putting Aurelia in prison would do nothing to save Blackthorn. The property technically belonged to Aurelia's mother and based on the financial picture that Aurelia had painted, the person named as executor of Aurelia's mother's estate would still have no option but to sell Blackthorn. So putting Aurelia in jail wouldn't stop the sale of the property.

So why would someone frame her?

It was possible that Aurelia had been framed by happenstance rather than intent. Had Lottie stumbled onto something that she wasn't supposed to see? Had her snooping on the grounds of Blackthorn put her in a position to learn something? Had someone killed her and then focused the blame on Aurelia simply because Aurelia was an easy scapegoat? It was possible.

Marcus slowed Diable to a walk, scanning the woods as he tried to sort through the knotted chain of events. The first thing he had to do was find Aurelia. He hated to tell her that he was the man responsible for keeping the legend of Blackthorn alive by playing Andre, but it was time she knew. He loved Aurelia. That meant that he could no longer deceive her, not even about Andre. It was time for her to learn all his secrets.

Once Aurelia was safely off the property, he intended to change into his regular clothes, contact Dru and get the sheriff and all the volunteers they could muster to come out to the estate and find the source of the crying baby. He was positive the sounds weren't made by a real infant, but he wanted no regrets.

Diable stopped, his attention concentrated on something in the woods that Marcus couldn't see. The horse began to dance, and Marcus used his legs and hands to calm the powerful animal. There was the sound of rustling, and Diable reared, front legs churning the air, as someone burst out of the woods.

"Joey!" Marcus said, leaning onto Diable's neck and urging the horse to settle back onto all four feet. "Where did you come from?"

Joey pointed back into the woods. "Miss Aurelia's in danger. I told her to go home. She wouldn't listen to me."

Marcus forced his voice to remain calm, gentle. "Aurelia's in the woods?" he asked.

Joey nodded. "She's looking for the baby."

"Is she okay?" Marcus pressed.

"Now she is, but she won't be for long if she doesn't leave." Joey walked up to the horse and began to stroke his neck. "Can I ride Diable?"

"Sure. Tomorrow. Listen, Joey, Yvonne is worried about you. She's been looking for you."

Joey's forehead furrowed. "Yes, she has. She's been looking all over for me."

"Maybe you should wait for me at the caretaker's cottage. When I find Aurelia, I'll come for you and take you back to town."

"No, I'm not going back there," Joey said. His frown disappeared, replaced by a grin. "I found something." He reached in his pocket and pulled something out. Taking Marcus's hand, he pressed something hard into the palm and then closed Marcus's fingers around it. "Take care of it," Joey said. "I found it."

Marcus opened his palm and looked at the cuff link that was there. It was gold and carved into an unusual design. "Where did you find this?"

"In the woods," Joey said. "I found it in the woods. I didn't steal it."

"Take it easy," Marcus said, touching Joey's hand on the horse's neck. "I know you don't steal, Joey. I just wondered where you found it."

"In the woods. Where that mean Mrs. Levert was killed. I found it there, but I didn't steal it."

Marcus knew that he had to be perfectly calm or he would agitate Joey more than he already was.

"It's okay, Joey," he said soothingly. "I know you didn't do anything wrong. It's okay." When he was sure that Joey had calmed, he nodded slowly. "Can you show me where you found the cuff link?"

Joey shook his head. "Not now. I'm scared."

Of all the places in the world, Joey was least afraid

of the Blackthorn woods. In fact, it was where he normally felt the safest. Marcus found his concern mounting, but he had to stay calm.

"Why are you afraid?" he asked.

"Mrs. Levert is dead. She won't ever wake up. She was snooping around Blackthorn and now she's dead. I don't want to die."

Marcus could imagine the trauma of Joey finding the woman's dead body. Undoubtedly, Joey was roaming around the woods of Blackthorn when Lottie was murdered. He must have stumbled upon the body.

"Was Lottie dead when you found the cuff link?" Marcus asked. He was frantic with the need for action, but he had to control himself.

"She was dead," Joey said. "She was lying in the woods. She wouldn't wake up. Then I saw the shiny thing in the dirt and I picked it up. I didn't steal it, I just picked it up in the dirt. I found it."

"Right beside Lottie?" Marcus asked, almost afraid to believe what he was hearing.

"Right beside her."

"Did you see anyone with Lottie?" Marcus asked. Joey shook his head. "No. I heard something. Moaning. But when I got there she was in the leaves. She was dead."

Marcus could see it all in his mind. If Joey had arrived a few moments earlier, he might have seen who actually murdered Lottie Levert. And he might also be dead.

"Climb up here," Marcus said, kicking the stirrup free and holding his hand out to give Joey a leg up.

"I can ride?" Joey was smiling again. "I love Diable. One day I'm going to ride him by myself."

"One day soon," Marcus promised as he helped the man up behind him and nudged Diable into a canter.

AURELIA CROUCHED IN the scrub brush and watched Joey climb onto the huge black horse. So the rider was flesh and blood, as was the animal he rode. And it was someone Joey knew and trusted—someone she'd once trusted with her heart and her future.

Aurelia tried to ignore the pain that hammered into her heart and head as she watched the horse and both riders gallop off down the road. She remembered the fleeting glimpse she'd caught of Andre as he'd ridden past her not an hour before. She'd recognized the profile, even though she hadn't admitted it to herself. Marcus. The man she'd given her heart to was the man responsible for keeping the legend of Andre Agee alive. Marcus was the man riding the estate in the dead of night, frightening away the teenagers who'd come to park and seek the treasure.

Marcus was the man who'd frightened her half to death on her first night at Blackthorn.

Marcus was the man who didn't want her to sell the estate.

She swallowed, fighting the sense of despair that swept over her.

Marcus was the man who'd betrayed her. All of the stories he'd told about Andre and the devil horse, all of the times he'd led her to believe that her great-great-great-grandfather haunted the estate.

And now she discovered that the only person haunting Blackthorn was him. No wonder he hadn't rushed to Blackthorn to help her hunt for Joey. He'd been busy changing into his costume and saddling his horse, preparing for his ghostly ride. But why? Why was Marcus haunting Blackthorn, frightening her? What was in it for him?

Marcus and Joey were long gone when she crept out of her hiding place and slowly began to make her way toward the driveway that would lead her to the highway. She would somehow make it into town. And when she was there, she'd go straight to Dru Colson and tell him everything she'd seen.

She hadn't gone ten feet down the path when she heard the mournful sound of the baby crying again. This time the sound infuriated her. Someone was playing with her, taunting her, and it was a good possibility it was another of Marcus's little games.

She started down the path, then paused. If she could find the source of the baby, she'd have the evidence she needed to prove to the sheriff that while she might be the heiress of Blackthorn, there were plenty of other people roaming the grounds.

Chapter Seventeen

Marcus lit a lantern and made Joey promise that he wouldn't leave the cottage. There was danger at Blackthorn, but Marcus didn't know the source of it. The safest place for Joey now was barricaded in the cottage—even if the power and telephone were out. Marcus had no doubt someone had cut the lines. He hadn't been able to complete his call to the sheriff, and he didn't have time to ride back to his car and drive to town.

"You'll be okay here, Joey," he said.

"I'm okay," Joey agreed. "Go find Miss Aurelia."

For all of his agitation, Joey knew every inch of Blackthorn, and he had a good memory of where he had been. He'd given Marcus an excellent idea of where Aurelia was. Finding Aurelia before someone else did was Marcus's primary goal.

"Lock the door and don't answer it unless it's me," Marcus said to Joey.

"I promise," Joey said, the agitation and fear gone

from his face and voice. "I'll be safe here. I love this cottage."

Marcus nodded. "You're safe. Wait here for me." He closed the door and waited for the sound of the dead bolt turning. When he was sure Joey had locked the door, he ran toward Diable. The horse was ground-tied by a huge magnolia tree. He was almost there when a dark shadow stepped into his path.

Marcus's fists came up, ready to fight. He couldn't see who the intruder was, but he wasn't expecting to meet a friend.

"I've come to help," John Ittawasa said calmly.

Marcus stopped, his fists slowly unclenching and his hands lowering to his side. "Why are you here?"

"The burial place," John said. "I want to protect it."

"By doing what?" Marcus asked, more than a little doubt in his voice.

"By helping Miss Agee. She isn't a killer."

"Aurelia will probably have to sell Blackthorn even if she's found innocent." Marcus knew that the Native American leader wasn't a fool—he'd thought it all through.

"And what will happen to the property if she's found guilty?" John asked. "Legally. What is the course of events for such property?"

"It belongs to her mother, who isn't competent. If there's no provision, the state will intervene and sell the property."

"Exactly," John said. "I'd rather take my chances

on Aurelia's disposition of the land than see it go into control of the state. There is too much room there for…error." The faintest smile crossed John's face. "Besides, I may never get another chance to work beside a ghostly legend."

Marcus had momentarily forgotten his outfit, but his stint as Andre Agee was over anyway. Aurelia was the only thing that mattered now. "Thanks, John. I could use some help."

"I've been here at Blackthorn for a while," John said. "Someone is in the woods. I've heard the crying baby. The sound moves around." He paused. "I believe it's a recorded sound and someone is moving a tape player all over the woods."

It was just as Marcus figured. "Why do *you* suppose someone would do that?"

"To frighten people away."

"Indeed."

"So someone is here tonight trying to frighten all of us away."

"All of us or Miss Agee in particular."

"Because someone wants the estate empty so they can hunt for the treasure." Marcus snapped the last piece into place.

"Yes, the treasure," John Ittawasa said with a good measure of sarcasm. "After all these years, the possibility of finding a treasure still tantalizes. Amazing."

"Most of the people who still hunt for the treasure are teenagers, kids looking for a little adventure. They hunt for the treasure and hope they won't meet Andre on his black horse.''

''This isn't the work of teenagers. Lottie Levert was murdered.''

Marcus felt the cuff link he'd tucked into his pocket. He had a solid clue to the identity of the murderer—or at least someone who was at the scene of Lottie's death. All he had to do was find the owner of the cuff link. And John could help him with that. He pulled it from his pocket and handed it to John, telling him all that Joey had said.

''It's a handsome piece,'' John said carefully. ''And expensive. Gold.''

''Aurelia is somewhere on the estate. Once I find her, the three of us can talk about this more,'' Marcus said.

''Find Miss Agee. I'm going after the crying baby. We'll meet back here,'' John said.

''Thanks for your help,'' Marcus said, putting his hand on the other man's shoulder.

''What's the old saying? 'Justice is its own reward.'''

EYES AND EARS alert, Aurelia made her way around the burial mound and to the drive that led back to the cottage. She clung to the shadows on the side of the path, taking care that she didn't reveal herself in the moonlight.

She was almost to the cottage when she heard the voices. She recognized Marcus's instantly, but she couldn't place the other voice. There was a strange inflection, a lilt that she couldn't identify.

She slipped closer, hoping to be able to distinguish what the two men were saying. Their voices were blurred by distance and she couldn't make out their words.

She was only a hundred yards away when she saw Marcus swing into the saddle. Before she could move, the black horse was flying toward her.

Panic overruled logic, and she whirled and began to run down the path. Fear made her run faster than she ever imagined, but behind her the horse was gaining on her. Marcus was going to run her down. She could almost feel the hot breath of the horse on the back of her neck. She was too afraid to turn around and see how close he was.

"Aurelia!"

She heard Marcus calling her name, but she had no intention of heeding him. Escape was her only salvation.

"Aurelia! It's me, Marcus!"

As if she didn't know. He'd betrayed her and she'd been an easy victim. The pain in her chest was more than her burning lungs. Her heart was breaking.

"Aurelia! Stop!"

This last was an order, and one she ignored. She ran with every ounce of strength and energy she had. The horse drew abreast of her.

"Aurelia, please."

She ignored the pleading sound in his voice. She

stared straight ahead, running. To her surprise, the horse bolted ahead of her. The ground shook as the big stallion spurted ahead.

Unbelievably, Marcus was leaving her alone. Just when she thought she was safe, she saw the horse whirl to a stop. Before she could stumble to a stop, Marcus was off the horse and standing on the ground. In another three seconds he'd closed the distance between them and swept her into his arms.

"Aurelia, it's me, Marcus. No one's going to hurt you."

She didn't even think. She swung as hard as she could, catching him in the chest. He staggered back but then recovered and pulled her against his chest, holding her so tightly she could barely struggle.

"It's me, Marcus," he repeated.

"I know who it is, you lying, conniving bastard." She couldn't help that she was crying. The sense of betrayal was too much.

"I should have told you I was pretending to be Andre. I'm sorry," he said.

"And what about the tape recorder with the baby? I suppose you're sorry for that, too. Let me go." She struggled again, but it only made him hold her closer.

"Did you find the tape recorder?" Marcus asked.

"I'm not the fool you took me for. Of course I found it. I'll admit, it was pretty creepy at first, but you sort of overdid it. I finally realized that no flesh-and-blood baby could have survived this past week without care and shelter. It was a good scam—the first time!'' Her fury ignited again and she stomped on his foot with everything she had.

Marcus jumped, hopping on his uninjured foot. ''I didn't have anything to do with the baby.''

''Sure,'' she said. ''Just another part of the play-acting legend. What did you hope to accomplish? That I would be frightened away from Blackthorn and forget about selling it? Well, you were wrong.''

''Aurelia,'' Marcus whispered, trying to smooth her hair with one hand while he held her with the other. ''Where is the tape recorder? Did you touch it?''

''What are you talking about? Did I touch it?''

''If your fingerprints aren't on it, the tape recorder may prove to be valuable evidence.''

''What kind of evidence?'' Despite her anger, Aurelia was beginning to listen to Marcus.

''Evidence that will help us find Lottie's killer.''

''As if you cared.'' She hated the fact that she wanted to believe Marcus. She hated her weakness, and she hated him for destroying her trust. ''Let me go.''

''Not until you listen to me,'' he said. ''Let's go get the tape recorder and I'll tell you all about Andre while we're on the way.''

''I'm not an idiot. If the tape recorder is evidence, why should I give it to you? You might destroy it.''

''Because I'm on your side, Aurelia. I know it looks odd, what with me dressed as Andre, but you have to trust me.''

"Trust you all the way to prison," she snapped, working to keep the tears out of her voice. He released his hold on her but kept her hand. In a moment she felt something hard pressing into her palm.

"What is that?" she asked.

"Can you see it?" Marcus waited while she held it up in the moonlight.

"It's a cuff link."

"Have you ever seen it before?"

She studied it more closely. "Wait a minute. I saw a cuff link like this the night of the ball. Let me think. It was…" her face drew into a frown.

"Who was wearing the cuff link?" Marcus pressed.

"Randall Levert."

Marcus lifted her onto Diable's back and swung up behind her. She was still regaining her balance when Marcus put the horse in a gallop. They were flying back down the drive to the caretaker's cottage. Once Aurelia had felt safe there, but now she had no idea who or what would be waiting for her. Worse than that, she felt she had never really known the man who held her in his arms as he guided the horse.

JOHN ITTAWASA was still waiting near the magnolia tree when Marcus stopped the horse and lowered Aurelia to the ground.

"What are you doing here?" Aurelia asked John in a voice that was none too friendly.

"He's come to help us," Marcus said.

"Us?" Aurelia asked in a challenging voice.

"Aurelia found the tape recorder," Marcus told John, ignoring her. "She didn't touch it. Once we recover it, we can take it to the sheriff for fingerprinting."

"Excellent," John said.

"Even better. Aurelia identified the cuff link." Marcus didn't bother to hide his excitement.

"Oh?"

"Randall Levert."

"I'm not surprised," John said. "Money is very important to him. As it was to his mother."

"What is all this about the cuff link?" Aurelia interjected.

Marcus could see that her patience had just about run its limit. The spark in her eyes was a warning that she was about to explode.

"Joey found that cuff link beside Lottie Levert's body," Marcus said, watching the reality of what he was saying dawn in Aurelia's eyes.

"When?"

"Shortly after she was murdered."

"But the cuff link belongs to Randall. Lottie was his mother."

Aurelia was having a hard time grasping that Randall possibly killed his mother. Marcus, too, found that concept difficult to accept. Especially if greed was the motive. To kill in self-defense or to protect a loved one was one thing. To kill for money—especially some imagined buried treasure—was something else again.

"I'm not saying Randall killed Lottie. I'm just saying that he was at the scene long before he burst into the sheriff's office and reported his mother missing."

He could see Aurelia thinking the chain of events through. "But Randall seemed genuinely concerned about his mother," she said. "I was there when he went to talk to Dru. He was...distraught."

"Or he was acting." Marcus let that hang in the air for a moment. "We aren't trying to convict Randall of anything, Aurelia. We just need enough doubt to clear your name."

"This is terrible," Aurelia looked over at John Ittawasa. "I'm sorry I was rude earlier. It's just that—" she glanced at Marcus "—I was badly deceived."

"I should have told you I was Andre," Marcus said quickly. Aurelia had softened a little, and if he was ever going to make her believe in him again, now was the time.

"You should have," Aurelia agreed. "But you didn't. Why not?"

"Andre has been so much a part of my life. I guess at first I felt a little silly confessing that I was acting like him—riding around Blackthorn on my horse. I just did it to keep the kids from ransacking the place, setting fires, destroying the burial mound."

"You should have told me," Aurelia insisted.

"I should have. I made a mistake."

"You nearly frightened me to death. Several times.

This evening, when I was hiding on top of the burial mound, I had the strangest sensation that I was somehow connected to old Andre, galloping around the estate.''

"And you are," Marcus said, taking her hands in his. "You are. I rode over here as Andre because I thought you might be in trouble. I believed that the surprise element might be of some benefit."

"Excuse me," John Ittawasa said. "We should recover the tape recorder before someone else does. Remember, if someone put it in the woods, they'll likely come back to claim it."

"You're right," Marcus said, squeezing Aurelia's hands one last time. "We can settle this later, when we both have time to talk. Just promise that you'll give me a chance to explain."

"I shouldn't." Aurelia took a deep breath. "But I guess I will." She looked around. "Where is Joey? I saw the two of you ride off."

"He's in the cabin, where I think you should stay," Marcus said. "I'm developing a plan, and I think it's going to be quite exciting."

"I'm developing my own plan," Aurelia said. "I'm a big fan of surprise endings, and I see one coming."

AURELIA WAITED in the cottage with Joey while the two men retrieved the tape recorder.

"Where did you find the cuff link?" she asked him. "Where exactly?"

"Right beside Mrs. Levert's hand. It was like her fingers dropped it when she died."

"Do you know what time you were there?"

Joey shook his head. "It was dark. I'd been walking in the woods, listening for the baby. I wanted to find who was making it cry like that."

Aurelia patted Joey's hand. "We'd make some cocoa if we had electricity."

"It's okay. I'm just glad you're here with me."

"I'm glad, too." Aurelia was surprised to find how fond of Joey she'd gotten.

"I'm sleepy," Joey said. "Can I sleep on the sofa?"

"Until Marcus returns," Aurelia agreed. "Then we'll go into town, I'm sure."

"I'm not going back to the church," Joey said, and his voice held such adamancy that Aurelia was surprised.

"Why not?"

"I don't like it there anymore."

"Why not?" Aurelia asked again. "What's wrong, Joey?"

"I don't like Mrs. Harris. She's mean."

"Was she upset with you because you didn't clean Mrs. Beckwith's garage?"

Joey shook his head. "No. She's mean about Blackthorn."

Aurelia patted his head. Joey loved Blackthorn as much as anyone could. But Yvonne Harris was simply trying to keep Joey from trespassing. "I'll talk to her and tell her that it's okay for you to come up here anytime you want as long as I'm here, okay?''

''Can I?'' Joey asked. ''You'll tell her?''

''I sure will. Now get some sleep.''

Joey was sleeping soundly when Marcus and John returned, the sophisticated tape player in their possession.

''It's set on a timer,'' Marcus explained. ''Very neat trick. I don't even want to think how they got a baby to cry like this.''

Aurelia shuddered. She didn't want to think about it, either. ''Maybe it's some type of audio you can buy.''

The lamplight made Marcus's features sharp. His eyebrows lifted. ''Good thinking, Aurelia.''

''The person who did this is very devious,'' John Ittawasa said. ''We must be careful.''

''I think we should turn this over to Dru and let him handle it from here,'' Marcus said.

''Absolutely not,'' Aurelia said, rising from her place at the table. ''I have a much better idea.''

''Oh, no.'' Marcus watched her as she leaned on the table so she was close to both men.

''Oh, yes. We're going to trial, just as if we haven't found anything. And during the trial, you can bring all of this evidence out and perhaps trick Randall into confessing.''

''That's a very bad idea,'' Marcus said abruptly. ''I don't like it at all.''

''Why not?'' Aurelia asked.

"Because if it doesn't work out like you imagine it, you could spend the rest of your life in jail. This isn't a television show, Aurelia. This is your life that's at stake."

"And I have full confidence that you can make a jury see how I was framed. We just need a speedy trial date."

"The grand jury meets next week. It's possible we can get a trial date in a matter of weeks," Marcus said. "We need at least that much time to prepare our case."

"And in the meanwhile, what happens to the real killer?" John Ittawasa interjected. "He remains free, possibly to kill again." He nodded to the sleeping form of Joey. "That young man may not be safe."

"Then we let the sheriff in on it," Aurelia said reluctantly.

"We'll see what Dru has to say once he prints this tape recorder," Marcus agreed.

Chapter Eighteen

Aurelia sat at the defense table as the judge banged his gavel for order. The trial was nearly half-over. The prosecution had almost finished presenting their side and judging by the expression on the faces of the jurors when they looked at her, Aurelia knew she was in deep trouble.

Marcus put his hand over hers, giving it a squeeze. He understood her fear. Even though they'd worked with Dru to solve Lottie's murder, Aurelia knew she was still risking a lot. Would the jury believe she was innocent? Probably not unless Marcus was able to get a confession from the real killer.

Dru had fingerprinted the tape recorder and found nothing. Though Marcus had shared the discovery of the cuff link and his idea of who killed Lottie with the sheriff, Dru had been unable to convince the prosecutor to halt the trial. Now it was up to Marcus to save her.

Randall Levert took the witness stand. The prosecutor examined him, emphasizing his testimony that Aurelia had threatened both him and his mother at the Mardi Gras ball. Aurelia watched Marcus's face and realized the prosecution was doing a good job of establishing motive.

When the prosecutor turned Randall over to Marcus, Aurelia held her breath.

Marcus asked a few easy questions. When Randall had relaxed a little, he struck.

"Tell us a little more about the ball where you say Miss Agee threatened you," Marcus requested.

"I've told you everything about it. She was dancing with me and then she said she was going to sell Blackthorn and no one would stand in her way. She said my mother was making trouble and that she would pay and so would I if I didn't stop my mother."

"That's very interesting," Marcus said easily. "Is Miss Agee a good dancer?"

Randall frowned and glanced at the prosecutor. "What does that have to do with anything?"

"It's a simple question," Marcus said. "Is she?"

"Yes." Randall glanced at the judge.

"What song did you dance to?" Marcus asked.

"I don't recall."

"Was it a tango, a fox trot, a—"

"It was a waltz," Randall said. "But I still don't see what this has to do with—"

Marcus cut in. "Did you hold Aurelia like this?"

And he struck a pose, left arm extended as if he held his partner's hand.

"Yes, I danced like everyone else."

"Thank you," Marcus said.

He walked over to the defense table and sent Aurelia a glance that made her heart beat faster. He was doing a masterful job of tying Randall into a knot.

Marcus picked up the cuff link from the table and took it to Randall. "Do you recognize this?" Marcus asked.

"Hey! Where did you get that? I've been looking all over for it."

"Then you admit it's yours?" Marcus asked.

"Yeah. I paid a lot of money for those cuff links. Where'd you get it?"

Marcus was smiling broadly when he asked that the cuff link be marked into evidence.

"What's going on?" Randall asked, turning to the judge. "Can he do that?"

"Please refrain from commentary or questions," the judge told him. "Just answer the questions."

Marcus asked a few more questions about the ball, then returned to the cuff link. "When was the last time you remember wearing your cuff links?" Marcus asked.

"At the ball," Randall said evenly. "Then I couldn't find one of them. Where'd you get it?"

"That'll be all," Marcus said, dismissing the witness.

He called Joey Reynolds to the stand next.

"Joey, do you recognize this cuff link?" Marcus asked him.

Joey nodded. "I sure do. I found it."

Marcus went over the details of where and how Joey had found the piece of jewelry.

Aurelia kept an eye on the jury. For the first time she saw doubt cross several of their faces. Marcus was leading them to rethink all the testimony they'd heard before. Two of them began to cut glances toward Randall.

Aurelia couldn't resist shooting a sideways glance at him, either. Just as she and Marcus had predicted, he looked bewildered, but that was quickly changing to belligerence as he began to see the trap they'd laid for him.

He started to rise, then thought better of it as he sat down, glancing back toward the spectators.

Marcus continued asking Joey questions, moving on to the day he'd disappeared from the church.

"I was at the church," Joey said, "but I left because I got scared."

"Scared of what?" Marcus asked.

The jury was now totally focused on Joey. Aurelia knew this was crucial and she kept her gaze riveted to Joey, trying to send him the strength she knew he needed.

"Mrs. Harris was upset."

"Because you didn't clean the garage you promised to clean, right?"

He shook his head. "She was mad at me. She

found my shoes outside and saw they were muddy. When she asked me how I got them dirty, I told her I'd been up at Blackthorn, looking for Andre.''

There was a brief ripple of laughter in the audience, but the judge quelled it with one harsh look.

''You were up at Blackthorn and what happened?'' Marcus said.

''I heard the baby crying.''

Marcus nodded. ''Just a moment, Joey.'' He came back to the defense table and Aurelia plainly saw the victory in his face. The testimony was going like clockwork. Marcus was tightening the noose, and Joey was making the perfect witness.

''A baby at Blackthorn?'' Marcus asked.

''Yes. I heard it crying in the woods.''

''Do you remember how the baby sounded?'' Marcus asked.

''I sure do. It was pitiful. I thought it was lost and hungry. That's why I wanted to find it.''

''Did the baby sound like this?'' Marcus walked to the defense table and pushed the button on the tape player. The plaintive cry of a baby in extreme distress filled the courtroom. Some of the female jurors gasped.

''That's it,'' Joey said. ''That's exactly what I heard. Where'd you find that?''

''I believe another witness will verify exactly where this tape player was found, Joey. But I have one more question for you.''

''Okay.''

"Why was Mrs. Harris so mad at you about going to Blackthorn?"

"Because I told her I found the cuff link and took it from beside Mrs. Levert's body. She was very mad about that."

"Did she want the cuff link back?"

Joey shook his head. "No. She said I never should have touched it."

"Thank you, Joey," Marcus said, turning him over for the cross. The prosecutor had no questions for him, and Joey took a seat in the courtroom.

Marcus called John Ittawasa to the stand and carefully detailed the events of the night the tape recorder was found by Aurelia in the woods at Blackthorn. Once John identified the tape recorder, Marcus had it marked into evidence.

"Why do you think someone was playing a tape of a crying baby in the woods?" Marcus asked.

Before the prosecutor could get his objection out, John had answered. "Someone was trying to frighten Miss Agee off the premises. We also found a large hole dug. It's my opinion someone is still searching for the legendary treasure of Andre Agee."

Aurelia exhaled a deep breath. Marcus's brilliant plan was playing out perfectly. He was asking exactly the right questions, leading the jury to the only conclusion possible—that she was innocent.

The prosecutor asked a few questions, establishing John Ittawasa's interest in Blackthorn and the burial mound, but he was unable to link John's interest with

Aurelia's. Marcus gripped Aurelia's hand as the testimony wound on.

"You're a genius at this, Marcus," Aurelia whispered to him. He glanced at her, his fear suddenly apparent in his eyes.

"I have to be," he said. "I can't lose this case. You can't go to prison."

"I won't," she said, gripping his fingers as tightly as she could.

When John was off the stand, Marcus called Yvonne Harris. The Realtor had been secluded with the other witnesses and hadn't heard any of the previous testimony. She glanced around the courtroom, her gaze lingering on Joey and deliberately avoiding the angry looks Randall was sending her way.

Aurelia felt her entire body tense. This was the crucial moment. All their hard work would either pay off or not. Yvonne looked completely at ease, and that was disconcerting.

As he had with Randall, Marcus softballed his questions at first. He established who she was and what she did. He asked her about the incident at Blackthorn that had scared her off the sale.

Laughing, she told him how she'd been followed in the woods by someone. "I was very frightened. It was probably Joey."

"You're sure someone was following you?" Marcus's expression was bland.

"I'm not prone to hysterics or wild imaginings.

There was someone in the woods, but I'm sure it was either a kid or Joey. I was silly to be frightened.''

"Would you like to see Blackthorn sold?" Marcus asked.

"I'd love to have that commission. But I also hate to see the old estate developed. It's such a historical landmark, as I'm sure you appreciate."

There was a murmur in the audience as that remark hit home. Marcus appeared unfazed.

"Yes, Blackthorn is a landmark. And one with a buried treasure. The last time you were there was when you went to look over the premises to sell it?"

For the first time, Yvonne looked tense. Her eyes narrowed and she glanced at Randall as if she wondered what he might have testified to.

"Yes," Yvonne said.

"Are you sure?" Marcus asked.

Yvonne froze. "Are you calling me a liar, Marcus?"

"I'm afraid I am, Mrs. Harris. You see, you were frightened at Blackthorn, but not so frightened that you didn't go back to the woods and plant this tape recorder." He picked up the player and held it up. "It's been identified already, but we have yet to name the owner."

A louder murmur swept the courtroom. The judge gaveled everyone into silence.

"Randall had one like it. It may be his," Yvonne said without turning a hair.

"Liar!" Randall jumped to his feet.

Yvonne stood up so abruptly the witness chair crashed into the wall. "Randall, you moron. What have you done?"

Randall's fists were clenched and his face contorted with anger. "You killed my mother! You said no one would get hurt. But you killed Mother, and then you took my cuff link. You left it where I would be blamed!" His face was red and he started forward toward the witness stand but a bailiff stepped into his path. "All along, you were planning on using me as the scapegoat! You were never going to share the treasure with me."

"Hush!" Yvonne ordered. "Sit down and shut up."

"You killed my mother and you were going to frame me! You're the one who told me to put the tape recorder in the woods and to keep moving it around. Now you've said it's mine." Randall looked at the judge. "It was all her idea. We didn't want Aurelia to sell Blackthorn until we found the treasure."

"You stole the hairbrush from the caretaker's cottage and used it to plant Aurelia's hair by Lottie's body, didn't you?" Marcus pressed Yvonne.

She didn't answer, and Marcus continued. "You never intended to kill Lottie, but when she found you digging for the treasure in the woods, there was an altercation. Things got out of hand. You struck her from behind, and then you panicked and killed her because you didn't want her to talk. What did Lottie see that was so important that she had to be silenced?'' Marcus continued.

Yvonne was impassive, and neither the judge nor prosecutor moved to stop Marcus. He took the opportunity to continue.

''Initially, you tried to frighten Aurelia out of selling Blackthorn immediately. Time was what you needed, wasn't it? Time. But Aurelia's financial needs didn't allow for more time. And once Lottie was dead, it was the perfect opportunity to complicate Aurelia's life, delaying the sale of Blackthorn indefinitely. You figured she would be cleared, but then Randall's cuff link would turn the focus of guilt on him. It was a brilliant plan, Yvonne. You'd get the time you needed and ultimately dump the partner you didn't want. The only aspect you didn't plan for was an innocent young man who stumbled onto the scene and removed the key piece of evidence you'd planted.''

Yvonne glared at Marcus but kept her mouth a thin line.

With a nod from the judge, Dru arrested Yvonne and Randall. Aurelia put her trembling hands on the table. She couldn't take her eyes off Marcus. He was superb. He'd brought the whole house of cards down, just as he'd promised.

''Miss Agee,'' the judge said in a solemn tone that stopped all the whispering in the courtroom. ''The charges against you are dismissed.'' He turned to the sheriff and the prosecutor. ''In my chambers, immediately.'' And then he was gone, his black robe flapping once.

Marcus rushed to the defense table, but Aurelia was quicker. She was in his arms, laughing and kissing him. ''You did it,'' she said. ''You forced the real murderer out.''

''I love you,'' Marcus said and then he turned to accept the congratulations of half the people of Natchez, including first and foremost, Ella and Joey.

MARCUS WATCHED AURELIA'S face as the old wooden cask was pulled from the ground. Ella and Joey were standing beside the deep hole that had been dug, and John Ittawasa was working the winch that slowly raised the old cask.

John gave Marcus a disbelieving smile. ''You were right. Ms. Harris had figured out where the treasure was really buried. When Lottie came upon her, she couldn't trust Lottie not to tell someone. That's why she killed her. And that's how you knew to dig in this location, wasn't it?''

''Once I realized what had really happened, it didn't take too much work to scout the area where Lottie's body was found. I knew Yvonne couldn't have moved the body far.''

''Then he began to think like Andre would think,'' Aurelia added. ''And after a couple of tries that didn't pan out, we hit the wooden case.''

''And soon enough, we'll know what's in it,'' John

said as he brought the cask level with them and began to swing it toward solid ground.

"None of this was ever about me," Aurelia said in a voice that still showed how much she was shocked by the turn of events. "Yvonne never set out to frame me or even to get rid of Randall. It was all about money."

"Greed is a powerful thing," Marcus agreed. "So what will you do with the Blackthorn treasure, Aurelia?"

"I don't know," she said. She pointed at the cask. "Probably wine turned to vinegar."

"Maybe not," Marcus said, putting his arm around her and squeezing. "Make me a promise."

"What?" she said, a little wary. In the weeks she'd spent in Natchez she'd learned that Marcus enjoyed a good practical joke.

"If there's treasure, you'll be my wife."

Aurelia began to tremble. "And if there is no treasure?"

"Oh, the penalty would be that you'd have to be my wife."

"Yes!" Aurelia said, throwing her arms around him. "Yes. I agree to the bet."

"I'll cater the reception," Ella offered. "We could combine the marriage with the reopening of your law office and kill two birds with one stone."

"None of you are very romantic," Aurelia complained, "but I'm going to work on all of you."

"I love to practice romance," Marcus said, then

kissed her soundly. When she was melting in his arms, he held her back. ''I think a handshake is more appropriate to seal a bet.''

''Oh!'' She hurled herself into his arms again, kissing him with passion.

''Then again,'' he said, ''who cares about tradition.''

''Hey! John has the crowbar!'' Joey was almost jumping up and down. ''Let's open it.''

Marcus, Aurelia, Joey, Ella and John gathered around the cask. It was old and almost rotted in places.

''It doesn't look very hopeful,'' Aurelia said. ''Remember, everyone, Andre gave all the money he took back to the rightful owners. It's not likely this will be anything of value.''

''You're forgetting that Andre had one of the finest plantations in the South. He could easily have made a fortune. Banks back then weren't all that trustworthy.'' Marcus said, getting a hammer to chisel off the rusty lock.

''Hurry up,'' Ella directed. ''We're dying from anticipation.''

''We are!'' Aurelia agreed. ''I've tried hard not to get my hopes up, but—'' She gasped as the lock fell apart and half the wooden chest fell away. The bright sun struck the gold coins. ''Incredible,'' Aurelia breathed.

Marcus felt his own knees get a bit rubbery as he

looked at the wealth. "I was afraid if we found anything, it might be Confederate dollars. Andre was smarter than that, though. I should have given him credit."

Aurelia and Ella knelt down, each picking up a gold coin.

"These are heavy," Ella said. "At least an ounce each."

"There are thousands of them," John said, also picking one up to examine it. "No telling how much they're worth."

"Is it enough to save Blackthorn?" Aurelia asked, looking up at Marcus. He felt the shock of her gaze and the sudden hope in her eyes.

"Enough to save Blackthorn, take care of your mother for the rest of her life and build a new life," Marcus said. He'd never been happier. The financial burdens that had weighed Aurelia down were gone. Andre had provided for his blood.

"Now you won't have to sell Blackthorn and you won't have to develop the land," John Ittawasa said with delight.

"You have my word that the burial mound will be protected," Aurelia said, rising to her feet. "Andre respected the burial mound, and I intend to do the same. I'll do better than that. I'll promise that no one will ever disturb this portion of Blackthorn. Somehow we'll figure out a way to make it legal."

John smiled at her. "That's a generous offer, but

I've been thinking. This mound could provide a tremendous amount of history about my people and how they lived. So much of my people's past has been lost. This is the resting place of a great king and as such, perhaps a team of professional archeologists should be allowed to examine it. Perhaps it will do for the Mound Builders what the pyramids did for the great pharaohs.''

"If that's your wish, then I'll honor it," Aurelia said.

"And can I really come here to live with you?" Joey asked.

Aurelia couldn't resist touching his face with her palm. "Yes," she said. "I'm going to build a new house here. Not a plantation house, but something wonderful and lovely. And you'll always have a place here, Joey, with me and Marcus." And she would move her mother to Natchez and place her in a top-notch nursing facility.

"Since you're granting boons and promises to everyone else, what about me?" Marcus asked. "I believe you promised to marry me."

"Not all the treasure in the world compares to a life with you, Marcus," Aurelia said, her face glowing with love.

"My question is, will the wedding come before the house building?" Ella asked. "This is February. I'd think March would be a good month for a wedding. All the azaleas and dogwoods and—"

"We could have it here, at Blackthorn," Aurelia said. "It would be the perfect ending."

"And the perfect beginning," Marcus said. "To a lifetime together."

*   *   *   *   *

Don't miss BABE IN THE WOODS,
the next book in
THE LEGEND OF BLACKTHORN *series,*
in June 2003, only from
Caroline Burnes and Harlequin Intrigue.

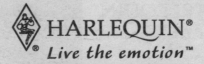

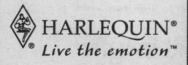

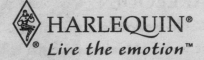

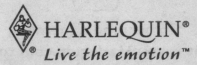